A DRIFTER'S FORTUNE

Love's a Gamble Book Two

KAY P. DAWSON

A Drifter's Fortune

Print version

© Copyright 2022 (As Revised) Kay P. Dawson

CKN Christian Publishing
An Imprint of Wolfpack Publishing
5130 S. Fort Apache Rd. 215-380
Las Vegas, NV 89148

www.cknchristianpublishing.com

Print ISBN 978-1-63977-207-0

CO-AUTHORS

Cissie Patterson
Ann Fiola
Cindy Nipper
Nancy Cowan
Mary Birchwood Lawson
Sharon McCluskey
Alice Robbins
Scott Sillars
Janet Hagan
Susan Poll
Tina Larson Carlson
Melissa Cowling Terry
Concetta Herigstad

Thank you to each and every one of you in my fan group who helped me write this book!

A DRIFTER'S FORTUNE

CHAPTER 1

"Now that I've got you all gathered together, it'd be remiss of me not to mention that I'm not particularly happy you're even hearing these words. Because if you're all sitting there listening to my old friend Henry read this letter, it only means one thing—I'm lying in a hole somewhere with my feet pointed to heaven and a mouth full of dirt."

Harrison held back his laughter as he listened to the letter being read to the group gathered in the lone saloon in town. Only Elijah Chance could manage to say the words so eloquently, even in death.

"You all know I was a bit of a betting man and I couldn't resist having a bit of fun now and then. It was also no secret I never found myself a woman to share my life with and have no kin to pass my fortune down to. I never stopped believing maybe a woman would have come *my way if I kept lookin', but I guess my tired old body had other plans.*

"So, I've gathered all of you, the men who live in this barren town of Romance, Kansas, together after you've laid me to rest. I have a proposition for any of you who'd like to take on the challenge.

"Women are scarce around here, that's no secret. Not many women want to live in a desolate town like this with nothing much to offer for luxuries and the thought of living on a ranch with some of the strangest creatures known to man would be enough to deter even the toughest of ladies.

"Here's the challenge, if you decide to take it. The first man who can get a woman out here to marry him will inherit my fortune. That includes all money and assets, including my beloved Last Chance Ranch.

"But, here's the catch... (You didn't think I'd make it easy on you, did you?) The woman must be a complete stranger to you and since we live almost smack dab in the middle of this great country of ours, she has to come from either the east or the west coast. Let's make her have to travel some to get here.

"How you get her here or convince her to marry you, is of no mind to me as long as you don't lie, cheat or do anything else illegal. And that means no abducting any woman against her will, Charlie."

Harrison and the rest of the men in the room turned their heads to grin at old Charlie Billings. Charlie wasn't the smartest man in these parts. He'd also been known to get himself in trouble now and then by bothering the women when he'd head into the much more exciting town of Abilene.

It was a running joke around town that the man would never find himself a woman without having to steal her away.

"You need to convince her to marry yo, and stay on the ranch with you. If she's stayed after a full six months without running for the hills, you've got yourself the title to the ranch. If she does decide to use her head and run as far away from here as she can get, then the race is on again."

His head started spinning as he realized the amount of fortune that was at stake here. Elijah Chance had a lot of money, more than most of them could likely even imagine. And the Last Chance Ranch he'd built from the ground up was a one-of-a-kind attraction that drew in even more money every year.

This wasn't a small settlement these men would be playing for. As Harrison looked around at the others, he noticed they all sat in shock at the opportunity that had been granted to them.

"In order to make sure everything is on the up and up, the wedding must be performed by Henry himself. He has to assure himself that the woman isn't being forced into anything without her consent, that the woman is unknown to the man, and that she will be treated fairly."

No one moved, no doubt considering how they

could convince any woman to come out to Romance. The name didn't reflect the town accurately at all and had only been named that by Elijah himself as he opened up the small settlement. He'd never married but always believed that romance, and love, was possible for anyone. He'd thought it would be quite funny to name the town after something completely out of character for the place.

He'd been an eccentric old man and Harrison was going to miss him. Even though he'd only worked on the ranch for a few weeks now, he'd gotten to spend a great deal of time with him and Elijah had a personality you didn't soon forget.

The truth was, the letter they were now being read by Elijah's oldest friend Henry, was no shock to him at all. He'd known the old man would make things fun and exciting right up until the end.

And, he always wanted to give everyone a fair and equal chance, including the animals he saved, giving them a second chance on the ranch he'd created to house them all. Over the years, he'd created quite a collection of misfit and wounded beasts who needed homes.

Now the ranch was an attraction that people came from all over to see.

He still had the usual animals that were expected on a ranch. In fact, he had one of the largest herds of cattle in Kansas. But his first love was the critters no one else wanted.

Harrison knew this was a huge opportunity. This was his chance to make his own fortune. He could end up bigger than the family who wouldn't accept him, never believing he was good enough to work in the family business or inherit any of the family fortune.

The Last Chance Ranch was his own chance for making his mark in the world, even if it was a bit off the beaten path.

It didn't matter. Elijah Chance had given him the same opportunity as the other men sitting in this room—to make that ranch his own.

All he had to do was find a woman, convince her to marry him, and move out to the middle of nowhere with a three-legged goat, a camel, a baby wolf and many other creatures that sent most women running the other way.

He was sure it couldn't really be that hard to do. He'd made his way from New Haven to Abilene by making impossible wagers that had men believing he was a fool and he'd always come out winning.

Looking up to the heavens, he let the old man know this was one bet he was willing to take.

CHAPTER 2

CHAPTER 2

"**P**ut this on your eye and it will help stop some of the bruising." Patience gently placed the cold cloth on her brother's eye.

"*Shhh!* You know if they hear you in here, you'll just be in as much trouble as me. Just go back to your room. I'll be fine."

Patience clenched her teeth tightly as she looked at her brother sitting on the bed, holding the cloth on his eye. He didn't wear a shirt and the bruises from this beating stood out prominently, plus the scars from previous ones. She swallowed hard, wishing she could just get them away from here.

"Mark, you're my little brother. And if I want to risk taking a beating to help you, then that's my decision. Now turn around so I can tend to the marks on your back from the strap."

Her brother's small back showed large, fiery red welts all the way across. A sob escaped as she saw how much damage there was this time.

"I swear, Mark, I will get us away from here." Her voice trembled as she tried to carefully wash the skin and offer it some coolness from the water.

"I'm the man and I'll figure out how to get us away."

She had to smile at her brother's attempt at being the man he believed he already was. However, he was three years younger than her; he'd just had his fifteenth birthday.

He always took the beatings, though, even if something was her fault. He never let them lay a hand on her, stepping between them and drawing their attention to him. It broke her heart that he did it but she'd done it for him for years when he was younger, so she knew he was now trying to repay her for the times she'd suffered for him.

Their parents had died when they were young and they had been taken in by relatives. No one had ever really explained the family connection but they went by the last name of the couple who'd raised them. Daniel and Andrea Thompson weren't nice people but, as far as they knew, they were the only kin they had left.

Patience couldn't really remember their parents, only vague recollections of memories that weren't clear in her mind. She sometimes thought she could hear her ma's voice or start to see glimpses of her pa's face in her memory but they always seemed just out of her reach. She'd only been four years old when they'd died coming out on the trail to Oregon. Her brother had only been a baby, so he had no memories at all.

She couldn't remember being brought to these relatives but, apparently, they'd been brought there by a family on the wagon train. And since the day they'd arrived, they'd been little more than free labor. They'd never been shown any love and Patience couldn't understand what they'd ever done wrong to deserve the mistreatment they endured.

But she'd had enough this time.

They'd almost killed her brother and she wasn't going to put up with it anymore.

"I'm answering the advertisement, Mark. This is our way out. Nothing can be worse than what we're suffering at the hands of Daniel and Andrea."

She'd been looking at advertisements in a paper that were looking for women to be mail order brides. Most of the notices were from men out in the west, where women were scarce.

But she'd been searching for one that would be as far away from the Thompsons as they could get and she'd found one yesterday that seemed perfect. However, whenever she mentioned it to Mark, he'd get angry, insisting he'd find a way for them to get away.

He didn't want her being put at risk by marrying a stranger.

"There's no other way. And I'm not waiting for them to kill one of us. You're getting to an age where they expect you to do so much and because you're getting bigger, their beatings are getting more severe."

Her brother was still small for his age and she had no doubt it was because they were given just the minimum amount of food they needed to survive. Also, Mark always insisted she have her fill before he did.

"No way, Patience. I'm not letting you end up in an even worse place than we are now."

Mark's voice shook with anger and frustration as she dabbed at the wounds on his back with a cold cloth. She didn't care anymore if he was angry with her. He may be the man in his eyes but she was the oldest.

It was time for her to step up and save them before things got even worse.

When she got back to her own cot, she pulled the paper out from beneath her pillow. She read the words once more that she knew were meant for her to see.

"Wife wanted immediately. No time for correspondence. All matters will be taken care of for your transportation to Kansas from wherever you are. Searching for a woman who isn't afraid to work, not afraid of animals of

any kind, and who will be willing to be married upon arrival, under agreement of staying at least six months. You will be treated fairly and have all of your needs met by a handsome man with a kind disposition. Money will be sent for your ticket on reply."

It wasn't giving her much to go on and sounded odd after reading some of the other advertisements which were asking for certain traits in the woman. They also provided a bit more information about the groom-to-be. Most notices wanted to correspond first to see if they'd be a good match before any money was sent. Mark said it sounded like something wasn't quite right with it but Patience, somehow, felt it was their answer.

For all she knew, he could be an old codger with no teeth, hair or money but, at this point, she didn't care if he was lying. If he treated them with even a small amount of kindness, it would be more than they were getting here with the Thompsons. And, if it was really bad, it sounded like she was only bound to stay for six months.

Maybe she could even get so lucky and find he truly was handsome and kind. Maybe she might even find someone who she could love and who would love her in return.

Somehow, she didn't really believe that could be true.

She shook her head to clear the wishful thinking as she pulled out some paper and a pencil to reply.

CHAPTER 3

"I still don't know if any amount of wealth and fortune is worth saddling yourself to a woman who may turn out to be a cranky old busybody...or worse. What will you do if she shows up here and ends up being an insufferable nag? You'll be obligated to spend, at the very least, the next six months living with her?" Lewis shook his head as he stood leaning against the rail outside his office.

Harris grinned at his friend. Lewis had been his friend since they were children back in New Haven. He'd had a bad run-in with a woman and headed west, landing as the sheriff in Abilene. As Harris had made his way west, determined to make his own way in the world, he'd found himself drifting toward the town where he knew his old friend would be.

Now, they stood outside Lewis's office, waiting

for the train that would be bringing Harris's bride. Since Romance, the small dusty town he now called home didn't have any train service running to it, he'd had to bring the woman to Abilene to meet her.

He knew the race was close and that there were a couple other men who had women arriving soon, too. He just hoped none of those women would be getting off this train.

He'd sent a message to Henry, telling him to meet him at the train station to carry out the ceremony that would give him the lead. The other men were free to marry the brides they'd sent for and hope Harris's bride would leave before the six months were up but he was already determined he wasn't going to let that happen.

He didn't care what kind of woman got off that train, as long as she was able to speak the words "I do" when the time came. After the six months were up, she could leave and he'd be willing to give her enough money to care for herself for the rest of her life.

"Well, I'm willing to take my chances. The ranch house is big enough that she can stay on one side and I'll stay on the other. I have no intentions of any kind of relationship other than business. Then she can be on her way and I can enjoy my ranch. And revel in the satisfaction that I made my own fortune without needing my family or my family name."

Lewis looked at him with an eyebrow raised. "You really think this is making your own fortune? I'd say it's more like a winning bet that paid out to the first man willing to throw his morals away and marry a woman for no other reason than money."

It was Harris's turn to lift his eyebrow toward his friend. "I'd think you'd know me well enough to know, I don't have a lot of morals anyway." His grin widened as he moved over and slapped his friend on the back.

"What will you do if this poor woman falls in love with you? Will you still send her away after the six months? Or, an even more intriguing development would be for you to fall hopelessly in love with her. Then what would you do?"

Harris laughed. "I'm not the kind of man who will fall in love with the first woman who smiles in my direction. Besides, like you said, I will likely end up with one who would rather grumble and complain every day of her life. And it's not like I'm exactly the type of man to have women throwing themselves at my feet, so I find it highly unlikely she'd fall in love with me."

This time it was Lewis's laughter that reached his ears. "I'd have to disagree with that statement."

Harris rolled his eyes. "You know what I mean.

They may be throwing themselves at my feet but not for the reasons I need."

The sound of the train's whistle cut through the air, making Harris turn toward the tracks across the street. "Henry better make it quick. I'm not going to let anyone else beat me to this prize. Not after getting this close."

He was going to be the first to marry and the one who would inherit the ranch for the six months. And after that, it would be his, free and clear.

He started across the street, not bothering to see if Lewis was coming with him or not. Other men mingled around and he wasn't taking any chances that one of them would beat him. He scanned the crowd, spotting Henry walking up the platform toward the train.

Moving as fast as he could, he caught up to him and grabbed him by the elbow. "Henry, glad you could make it. Let's go get me hitched."

The older man smiled. "Somehow, I knew it'd be you who won."

"He hasn't won yet. He still has to convince the poor woman to spend the next six months with him, on a ranch in the middle of nowhere, with animals that leave a lot to be desired." Lewis had walked up behind them, obviously intent on making his wedding day as miserable as he could.

"Now, Lewis, no need to be such a grump on my wedding day. I'm sure someday you'll find some poor soul who will agree to marry you too." He couldn't help grinning as he watched Lewis cringe.

"Not likely," he grumbled.

Harris stood with the other men, watching as the train slowed down, then came to a stop with a hiss. The smoke from the engine settled around them as they waited for the door to open and the conductor to let the passengers off.

His mouth was dry and his heart started beating hard in his chest. Had he thought this through enough? Tying himself to a complete stranger, even if it was for only six months, was just about the most foolhardy thing he'd done in his life. And he'd been known to do a lot of those.

What would he do if she was a horrible person, who made every waking moment miserable? Would it be worth it?

He swallowed against the dryness in his throat, trying to calm his suddenly tight nerves.

The door finally opened and the conductor reached up to start helping the passengers off. The first few people off the train were older women obviously traveling together as they chatted the entire time, not even bothering to say a word to the conductor.

A few men stepped down, and with each person who stepped onto the platform, his heart beat harder against his chest.

What if she'd missed the train? What if she'd taken his money and run?

Just as he thought there was no one left and he could feel a panic begin to swell in his gut, the conductor reached in to the compartment with a large smile covering his face.

He said something to the passenger as he watched a woman's hand reach out to take his. If Harris didn't know better, from where he stood, it almost looked like the man was blushing.

A small woman stepped out, holding her other hand up to shield her eyes from the sun. She held her head high, looking around as though searching for something, or someone.

His heart lurched as he realized he was looking at his bride.

He couldn't see much of her hair but the few wisps he could see poking from beneath her plain bonnet were brown. Her dress wasn't anything to look at and he thought perhaps it had been patched more times than could be possible.

Just as he thought she was about as plain as the dress she wore, her head moved to look to where the men stood on the platform. Her eyes were the brightest blue he'd ever seen and they seemed to pin him where he stood.

He tried to look away, or move toward her, or do anything to stop himself from standing with his jaw hanging to the ground. Before he could move, she smiled at them and his heart stopped beating.

He almost fell over as Lewis slapped him hard on the shoulder, his laughter reaching his ears. "Sure glad you aren't the kind of man to fall in love with the first woman who smiles in your direction."

CHAPTER 4

Patience saw the men standing on the platform and immediately felt her eyes drawn to the man with the dark hair and eyes that matched. He almost looked like he was scowling but at least the two men beside him were smiling.

She nervously patted at her worn skirt as she stepped down, wishing she could have had something nicer to wear to meet her new husband. But this was the best she had, so she'd mended it and tried to make it as presentable as she could.

Her eyes moved to the two older ladies who had stepped from the train ahead of her. She'd admired them along the way, how poised they were and so proper. Their dresses were of the finest silks and lace and they looked like they didn't have a care in the world.

A knot formed in her stomach as she realized

the man who was frowning at her was likely disappointed. For some reason, she already knew he was Harrison Winchester, the man she was meeting. And he'd just watched her come from the train looking like she was wearing a flour sack that had been patched together.

The Thompsons had never spent any money on her or Mark and the dresses she had were old cast-offs that had belonged to Andrea Thompson while Mark got the worn, hand-me-downs from Daniel.

If Harrison was disappointed in his new bride, she could only imagine how he was going to feel when he saw her brother step out.

She hadn't mentioned she had a brother coming with her, worrying that he'd say no or wouldn't still want her to come. So she'd taken some of the money the Thompsons had hidden under their mattress and used it for her brother's ticket.

She knew it was wrong to steal but she didn't know what else to do. There was no way she was leaving him there and they'd never received any money for any of the work they'd done over the years. The way she saw it, they owed them at least that much.

"Wait for me, Patience. You're not getting out there without me to make sure no one accosts you or dares to try anything with you." Her brother's angry voice reached her ears as he hurried to step out behind her. She knew he looked a little rough around the edges but she hoped Harrison wouldn't turn them away now that they were here.

Watching his face, she worried he was about to do just that.

Not only had he just ended up with a plain woman for a wife but he was about to find out she came with a stubborn and angry younger brother.

Lifting her chin, she pushed her shoulders back and made her way toward the men. The older man pulled away and came to meet her, with his hand outstretched for hers.

"You must be Patience."

She felt her eyes widen as he bowed toward her, then lifted her hand to kiss the back of it. She'd seen women being treated like that before but they were usually women of status. She'd never had a man bow to her and treat her like royalty.

She decided she liked this man immensely.

"I'm Henry Northcott." He pulled her toward the two younger men. "This is Lewis Kinkaid, one of the working sheriffs here in Abilene." The sheriff's smile covered his face as he nodded his head at her.

"Nice to meet you, Patience."

Henry still held her elbow and he nudged her toward the other man who still hadn't spoken a word. "And this man, who doesn't know how to use the manners God gave him, is your soon-to-be husband, Harrison Winchester."

Her heart leaped into her throat when the man finally smiled at her, lifting her hand to place a kiss on it too. "Sorry for being so rude, I was just a bit shocked. I'd expected someone a little different, I suppose."

She felt her own smile falter at his words, realizing he was truly disappointed in her. She knew she wasn't the kind of woman to turn most men's heads in her direction but she'd hoped he could see past that.

Before she had a chance to dwell on it, her brother pushed her aside, coming to stand between her and Harrison.

"I don't know what your plan is, or why you brought her out here, but I'm telling you right now, I'll be keeping an eye on you. If you raise even so much as one finger in her direction, you'll answer to me."

She cringed as she saw Harrison crease his eyebrows together in confusion, backing up to put some space between them. Her brother was nowhere near as big in stature as Harrison but it didn't seem to deter him in any way.

"And who are you?" Harrison crossed his arms in front of him.

"I'm her brother, that's who."

Harrison turned his eyes to look at her with a raised eyebrow. "You brought your brother? That wasn't agreed on. And I certainly didn't expect to be paying for two tickets. The extra money I'd sent you was to take care of your needs along the way."

"No, I didn't use your money for his ticket, I promise. In fact, I have some left over I will be able to give back to you. But I had to bring him with me. He's the only kin I have and I hoped maybe he could find work out here. He won't be any trouble at all." She turned her gaze to glare in her brother's direction. "Will you, Mark?"

Her brother was still staring down Harrison. "I won't cause any trouble if he doesn't ask for any."

"Henry!" A man's voice shouted from the other end of the boardwalk. "Henry, I have a woman here willing to marry me."

She watched as Henry turned to Harrison. "Guess you better hurry up and decide if this is worth arguing about at the moment."

She wasn't sure what was going on or why another man was trying to let Henry know he was getting married too.

Before she could think about it any more, Harrison tucked her hand into the crook of his arm and turned her to face Henry. To her horror, she saw a hole in the finger of one of her gloves and hurriedly removed them.

"Not at all. You better be ready to speak fast." Harrison looked in her direction, giving her a smile and a nod of his head.

"Time to get married, Patience."

"You mean right now...here?" She would have liked to at least wash the dust from her travel-weary face and perhaps put a brush through her hair.

"I'm not waiting. And, something you'll learn about me while we are together, the very virtue you're named after is something I'm sorely lacking in."

Her head spun as she heard Henry start to say the words that would marry her to Harrison. The other man who'd shouted earlier was still hollering and he was getting closer.

But all she could hear was Harrison's voice saying he would take her to be his wife. She didn't dare argue and ask to wait for a better time, so she repeated the vows she was required to say, then almost fainted as she heard Henry's voice proclaim...

"You may kiss your bride."

CHAPTER 5

He looked into the blue depths of the eyes staring back at him and almost laughed at the sheer terror he could see in them. Her eyes bulged and he was certain she hadn't blinked since Henry spoke the words.

Something about the way she held herself, determined to be the dutiful wife as she'd agreed to be but still so afraid of what had just happened, caused him to hesitate. He didn't want to scare her any more than she obviously already was.

He leaned closer and lifted her hand to his lips once more. "We have plenty of time for that." He gently placed a kiss on the skin there and, this time as he held her hand, he could feel the calluses that covered her small palms.

He turned them over, examining them for a

brief second before she pulled her hand away and wiped them on her skirts.

What life had this woman had to endure before now?

The man who'd been yelling for Henry had made it over just as the ceremony was finishing.

"Harrison Winchester, you haven't won yet!" The voice rumbled across the wooden planks of the platform they stood on.

It was Dirk Marley, the one man Harrison had vowed he would not let beat him. The fact that he'd come that close irked him.

"Sorry, Dirk, looks like you're just a moment too late. I'm a married man now." He knew he shouldn't be gloating and egging the other man on but he'd never liked Dirk. And the fact that he'd kept him from getting his hands on the fortune left by Elijah Chance thrilled him more than he was willing to admit.

Dirk had never been good to the old man and had been one of the laziest ranch hands around. Now, Harrison would be his boss.

He finally noticed the lady Dirk had dragged over from the train. She was stunning. Her hair was the color of gold and it hung in perfect curls over her shoulders. She was wearing a dress that perfectly matched the green of her eyes and there wasn't a wrinkle to be seen.

He caught Patience looking at the woman with a

smile on her face before she reached her hands down to pat at her own threadbare skirt.

But the thing Harrison noticed the most was the way the other woman's eyes were wide and her jaw clenched in anger. She put a tight smile on her face as she looked at Patience. "Well congratulations, looks like you're a wealthy woman. If you can stand to be out on that filthy ranch, that is."

Harrison narrowed his eyes as the couple strode away. Something about this woman, and the way she spoke, led him to believe she wasn't entirely unknown to Dirk.

But it didn't matter to him one way or another. He was married and now all he had to do was convince Patience to stay the next six months. Although from the look of her, he decided she likely didn't have anywhere else to go anyway.

Her brother was growling behind Patience, trying to push her out of the way. She was trying her hardest to stop him. "Mark, stop! You knew this was what I was coming out here for."

"Not the minute you stepped off the train! What kind of barbarian forces a woman to marry a complete stranger without so much as even letting her have a drink of water first?"

Harrison took a good look at Patience and realized he hadn't given her the warmest reception upon arrival as he should have done. Black shadows dusted under her eyes and her cheeks were overly red.

He'd been so caught up in the brightness in her eyes, he hadn't noticed anything else.

Lewis and Henry both moved over and Harrison watched Henry put his hand out to soothe the boy. "You're right, young man. We haven't been civilized at all. We will remedy that right now."

Harrison looked between the two of them. "Where are the rest of your bags?" He'd seen her carrying a small beat-up bag and the brother had a sack slung over his shoulder.

As he spoke, he watched her chin go up. "These are all of our bags, Mr. Winchester."

He fought from rolling his eyes. "Maybe you're used to calling men by the more formal term but around here, it's not necessary. We're married now, so I'd say you can call me Harris as my friends do. If you call me Mr. Winchester, I won't be inclined to answer."

He reached down and picked up the tattered bag, suddenly feeling furious at whatever conditions she'd been living in. Yet, she carried herself with a regal air that if you didn't see her clothes and her belongings, you'd be sure she'd walked straight from the ballrooms in London.

"Don't you have any more dresses or clothes?" He knew he wasn't being very tactful with his questions but, the truth was, he was irritated that he'd only been married a few minutes and was already dealing with issues his new wife had brought with her.

He could see her throat move as she swallowed hard and she placed her hand on her brother's arm. He'd stepped forward, cheeks glowing red and ready for a fight. She just shook her head and held him in place.

"I have everything I need right here. The dress I'm wearing is just fine and, I assure you, I won't ask you for any money to replace it. In fact..." She reached down into the small reticule she held and pulled out some bills, then tucked them into his hand. "That's the rest of the money you sent to get me here. I wanted to make sure I didn't overstep and use any I didn't need after you'd been kind enough to send me the money for the ticket."

Harrison stood, unable to move, holding the few bills in his hand, the other holding her bag. He didn't even know what to say. The amount of money he held in his hand was nothing, especially compared to what she could have used it for.

Something inside him tightened. Ever since he was a young boy, when he mentioned the Winchester name, women had chased him, believing he'd be able to give them access to the family riches. No one had ever seen him for who he was.

But this woman in front of him had nothing, yet

she'd made sure she repaid him the extra she believed he was owed. Riches didn't seem to be important to her at all.

He lifted his head and met her eyes. She was smiling and he had to fight the urge to apologize to her, sure she deserved a better man than he was. Someone who wouldn't be prepared to go so far as to marry a complete stranger just to get his hands on a fortune.

He could see Lewis staring at him intently, shrugging when Harrison met his eyes. Obviously, he was feeling just as confused that a woman wouldn't use money she was given when it was freely offered to her.

"Henry, how long until I can get my hands on some of the money?"

"Well, we could head to the bank now..."

"Good, I need enough to get my bride a new wardrobe and some clothes for her brother." He could see she was going to argue, so he just took her hand in his and started to walk toward the bank.

He'd promised himself he wouldn't let his feelings get carried away over any woman who came to marry him. But he worried that he may have already crossed that line before they'd even left the platform in front of the station.

CHAPTER 6

"You really didn't need to do that Mr. Winchester...sorry! I mean, Harris." She quickly corrected herself when he turned his head and scowled at her. "I feel just awful that you felt the need to get clothing for Mark and me. We truly would have been fine. We've made do with what we have for a long time now."

She was embarrassed about her lack of decent dresses and was ashamed that he'd had to already spend a small fortune getting clothing for them. He'd insisted she needed some sturdy skirts out on the ranch and simple blouses. Some of the items were in stock but there were a few which would have to be made.

She could feel heat rush to her cheeks again as she thought back to when the lady had asked about "underthings." Patience really only had the bare minimum but how could she admit that in front of Harris?

But he'd simply waved his hand and acted like it wasn't a big deal, saying to make her ten of everything she would need.

Mark hadn't been co-operative at all and had fought against everything Harris tried to do.

She kept her hands clenched in her lap, the bouncing of the wagon jolting her spine with every rut they hit on the road. "And I'm sorry I never mentioned my brother would be coming with me. I just worried that you wouldn't want him coming too and I couldn't leave him behind."

Her brother was sitting in the back, arms crossed in front of him and a scowl set on his face. He wasn't making anything easy for any of them.

She felt like she needed to explain to Harris but he wasn't saying anything either, just staring ahead at the road as they drove the wagon back to the small settlement he'd told her was called Romance. She'd laughed to herself when she heard that, thinking what a strange name it was for a tiny town in the middle of nowhere as Harris had described it.

But it was now her home, so she was ready to embrace it and make it a place she would love.

He'd also said it would be at least a half a day's travel to get there, so if there was anything else she needed in town, she should speak up before they left.

After everything he'd already bought for her, there was nothing she could imagine she'd ever need.

Deciding he mustn't be in much of a talking mood, she let her eyes fall on the landscape around her. There were fields of green and gold as far as she could see. Hills moved up, then fell down into small valleys and trees dotted the land around them.

The air was warm on her face, and she let her eyes close as she tipped her head back and took in the smell of the fresh air. She hadn't gotten out of Portland very often growing up, so she hadn't had many opportunities to see anything quite this breathtaking.

"So, what's your story? Why were you willing to leave your home and come out here to marry a complete stranger, knowing it quite likely wouldn't even be a permanent arrangement?"

His voice startled her and she whipped her head forward as she opened her eyes and caught him looking right at her.

His eyes were dark and she found herself struggling to find words as he held her gaze. She turned to look back out at the fields, deciding it would be much easier to concentrate that way.

"I don't have a story, really. My parents died when I was just a girl, on our way to Oregon on a wagon train. From what we were told, another couple cared for us until we got to Portland, where we were given to family who took us in and raised us." She swallowed hard against the dryness of her throat. Talking about her past always hurt. She wished she could remember more of her parents, but her vague memories only came to her in her dreams.

"The couple who raised us weren't nice people and we were nothing more to them than servants who helped them take care of their boardinghouse and stables in town."

She knew there was no sense trying to lie or make her past out to be more than it was because he'd be able to see right through that. The clothes she wore gave it away. She turned to look at him again, her heart skipping a beat when she saw him still watching her so intently. She was beginning to think his eyes could read everything she was thinking.

He tipped his head back, motioning toward her brother. "That why he's so angry?"

She peeked back at her brother who was watching the landscape around them but pretending not to be happy about it. Something in his eyes shone through, though, and she saw a spark of hope she hadn't seen for a long time. It warmed her heart to see it.

Turning back to look out past the horses tied to the wagon, she shrugged. "He didn't have an easy time with the Thompsons. As hard as they always were on me over the years, they were worse to him. He has spent his life trying to protect me and worrying when he couldn't. And he's angry that he wasn't able to get me away from them. When I said I was answering your advertisement, he felt like he'd let me down," She kept her voice low so only Harris could hear her.

They came around a bend in the road and, in the distance, a long winding lane led up to a large ranch house. There were buildings spread all around the sprawling property and animals moved about in different pens set up on the grounds. She assumed they would be the cows and horses that made up the ranch.

It looked breathtaking. There were small hills rolling in the back of the property as far as she could see and a creek making its way through the trees. She couldn't believe this would be her home.

She turned her head slightly to look at Harris, seeing him smile as he looked all around the land before them. He obviously felt pride in what he owned.

As they got closer, the animals moving around were easier to see and her eyes squinted. Surely she was seeing things.

That couldn't possibly be a camel!

But as they made their way up the dirt lane, her chin dropped as she saw that it was indeed what she'd thought. And in a pen farther up, she saw an animal that looked like a buffalo.

A goat came running toward them from near the house and she could see it only had three legs. Right beside the goat was a yellow dog, who seemed to be following closely, as though he was being led.

What was she seeing? She couldn't see any horses or cattle anywhere. Her head snapped around to look at Harris, who was watching her with a grin covering his face.

"Welcome to the Last Chance Ranch, Patience. A place for all kinds of beings who need a little extra care while they heal. Some will never leave and some will move on when they feel they're ready. There's no other place like it in the world."

Patience started to feel the dirt in the back of her throat as her mouth still hung open. She slowly turned her eyes and looked around again as they came to a stop.

Watching the three-legged goat and the dog she could now tell was blind make their way to the wagon, she suddenly felt a peace she hadn't felt before.

Somehow in her heart, she could believe there really was no other place like it in the world.

For her and her brother, it truly was their last chance.

CHAPTER 7

"Henry, don't you have someone else you could be bothering right now?" Harrison wasn't in the mood to have the older man on his heels, questioning and nagging him about everything.

Henry had been friends with Elijah for many years, long before Harrison showed up on the ranch. He'd often wondered why the old man didn't just leave his ranch to his friend since neither of them seemed to have any other family that he knew of.

He'd heard some of the ranch hands talking about Henry having a wife who had died a few years back and a daughter somewhere, but other than that, Elijah and Henry had been two bachelors who founded Romance and set up the ranch using the fortune Elijah Chance already had.

Elijah owned it and Henry was content to run it.

"Just want to make sure you remember that no

amount of money is worth it if you hurt someone along the way. That girl and young boy have been through a great deal, that much is apparent. Have you explained to her the terms you've decided on? Does she know you only plan to keep her here for the six months?"

Henry hadn't been happy with his decision to only have the woman stay for the six months as set out in the will to receive the fortune and he'd been a thorn in his side since he'd mentioned it. He said he didn't think that was what Elijah had in mind when he'd come up with this plan for his legacy.

He believed he should at least give her a chance to see if they could have a true marriage.

"I've mentioned it to her, I think. I'm sure I even put it in my notices. Besides, she will be well taken care of and away from the relatives who've treated them so horribly. I wouldn't just send her away without anything." He ignored the niggling of guilt he was feeling, knowing he likely hadn't explained everything to her as well as he should have.

And after seeing her step off the train in the tattered dress, he knew she'd been running from something with a hope for a better future. He could still give her that. It just wouldn't likely be what she was hoping for.

He was going to make sure she never had to

worry about money or struggling to survive again, so surely that would be enough.

But for some reason, something kept tugging at him as he sensed she didn't care at all about money. She seemed to be content with anything she was given and was just happy to be away from the family she'd left behind.

He couldn't stop thinking about the blue eyes that had turned to look at him when she stepped onto that platform.

"Something tells me that girl is hoping for more than just money. No matter what you've told her or what she even expects from this arrangement, you know as well as I do she deserves better. She should have the chance for someone to care for her, to look after her and make her feel loved."

Harrison lifted his head from the hoof he was working on to look at Henry. "Henry, you're sounding like an old softie."

Henry just shrugged. "I just know a lonely soul when I see one. And Mark needs a guiding hand to show him the world isn't the horrible place he believes it to be. This could be your chance to make a difference for both of them."

Harrison bent his head, setting the horse's foot back on the ground. "I'm not the kind of man that can make any difference in anyone's life. You know that as much as I do, Henry." Standing up, he pushed the stool back he'd sat on and walked over to the barn door. He strode out into the daylight and raised his gloved hand to shield his eyes from the bright sun.

"So you've made some bad choices in your life. There's not a man alive who can say they haven't done the same. But the difference is, you're working now to right your wrongs and you're determined to be a better man. Couldn't ask for much more than that, I'd expect."

Harrison turned and shook his head as he looked at Henry. "Henry, I appreciate your advice but I have a ranch I need to run and this is my first day as boss around here. I need to make sure everyone knows how I do things and standing around here chatting with you isn't going to help."

He'd already sent word to the bunkhouse for all of the ranch hands to meet him outside first thing. He didn't think it would look good for him to be late when he was hoping to earn their respect.

Some of them were angry that they hadn't won, so he already had to deal with that. And some didn't think he knew enough about running a ranch to be willing to show him any respect. After all, a lot of these men had worked here for years and certainly longer than he'd been here.

He'd been the last man hired on to work here before the old man died.

He had an uphill battle if he expected to get the men working for him without causing any problems.

Dirk had already been raising a ruckus, getting back to the ranch before him yesterday.

While he'd been getting clothing for Patience and Mark, Dirk had ridden ahead and made sure everyone knew who the winner was. And he'd also made sure to rile the others up to a point of almost having a mutiny by the time he'd gotten back.

He wasn't sure what Dirk had done with the woman he was supposed to marry but he didn't waste too much time thinking about it.

He strode toward the bunkhouse, prepared for a fight. He didn't want to admit it but he was secretly glad to hear Henry's steps following behind. Somehow, the older man always seemed to be able to reason with the others when no one else could. Everyone respected him. He'd been working on this ranch since the day it had been founded.

He had his own small house on the outskirts and was the one man everyone else took orders from. Henry was a preacher but he was also the best ranch boss in the area. No one would say anything against the man and if you treated him with respect and kindness, he'd give it back.

He gave the Sunday service in the small settlement every week, then came back out to work on the ranch with the others. It's the way it had always been done, so no one ever questioned it.

Harrison walked around the small chicken house that sat next to the bunkhouse. He was ready to prove to these men that he was their boss now and they had to respect that or move on.

He wasn't going to let them make him feel like he wasn't capable of running this ranch. He may be the new one around here but he'd won fair and square. Now, it was his turn to prove his own worth in the world, away from the Winchester name.

As he looked at the faces on the men staring back at him, lined up along the bunkhouse, he realized getting Patience here and marrying her was likely the easiest part of winning this fortune.

CHAPTER 8

Patience looked down at the skirt she wore, still feeling her heart swell with happiness when she felt the soft fabric that had no holes or tears. She spun around while looking in the small mirror she'd found over the wash basin, letting herself have a moment to enjoy the feeling of having something of her own to wear.

All she could ever remember was being given the worn remnants of the dresses Andrea Thompson was done with. Harrison had bought her this dress to wear and she knew she'd treasure it forever.

She stumbled mid-turn as she saw the man she was thinking about standing in the doorway of the kitchen watching her. He had his head tilted to one side but she thought she could see a small smile tugging at his lips.

"Oh, Harrison. You startled me. I didn't hear

you come in." Her voice was breathless as she tried to hurry back over to the stove to stir the pot she'd set on to cook.

"That's all right. And, I told you to call me Harris. That's what most people around here call me anyway." He walked over and washed his hands in the basin, then turned and leaned against the cabinet. "I told you I could make the lunch today to let you and your brother have a chance to get settled in better."

She hurried to grab a cloth, then bent to take the biscuits from the oven. "I know. But I wouldn't feel right lying around doing nothing while you've been out working. It's the least I can do for everything you've already done for me." She had been told part of her duties as ranch wife would be to feed the men lunch and dinner. He'd told her the men cooked their own breakfasts out in the bunkhouse.

She was the only woman on the ranch, along with Harris, Henry, Mark, and six other men who worked and lived out here. She'd been anxious to prepare the meal, wanting to show Harris that she was more than capable of cooking for that many people. After all, she'd been doing it at the boardinghouse for years.

She took some bowls down from the shelf, then turned to set them on the table in the middle of the room.

"Here, let me take those." She jumped as she realized Harris was standing right behind her, and she ran right into his chest. Thankfully, he was able to grab hold of the bowls before they crashed to the ground.

"Sorry, didn't mean to startle you again." He had a lopsided grin and as she looked in his face, she was able to see his dark eyes up close for the first time. Her heart gave a flicker as the scent of leather and musk reached her nose.

He moved over and started laying the bowls on the long table. Each side had a bench that ran along it and both ends had a chair. She wondered where she would be sitting.

"After everyone is finished eating, I could take you around to show you the ranch if you'd like. I reckon since this'll be your home, at least for the next few months, it'd do you good to know where everything is, and what all we have here."

"Yes, I'd like that very much, thank you, Harris."

She was feeling uncomfortable, still not certain what her role around here was to be. She knew he'd mentioned several times that she wasn't required to stay after six months but she still didn't quite know what he meant by that.

When they'd gotten home yesterday, it had been late in the day, so Harrison had shown her and Mark their rooms, then told them he had to get out to take care of his chores. They'd been left alone to settle in, where she'd spent the evening sitting on the edge of the soft bed wondering if he'd been disappointed in her.

She hadn't known if they would be a true married couple and share a bed when she'd arrived, and she worried that he hadn't been happy when she stepped off the train.

But at least he'd still married her and not sent her away with nothing.

She had hope that perhaps over time they could build a future together.

The sound of loud voices coming through the door brought her thoughts back to the present and she quickly placed the biscuits on a plate and set them on the table. She raced back to the stove to pour the stew she'd made into a large serving bowl. As she lifted it, she suddenly felt the heavy load lighten. Harris had lifted it from her hands and moved to pour it into the bowl for her.

She stood looking at him, unsure what to do. No one had ever helped her with something so simple before but, for some reason, it warmed her heart. He hadn't even realized he'd done anything out of the ordinary.

He flashed her a smile, then turned to carry the bowl to the table.

She picked a cloth up from the cupboard, then started to place the pots and utensils she'd dirtied into the large basin she'd already put warm water in.

She didn't want anyone to see how nervous she was feeling. Her brother walked out from down the hall and she watched as he sauntered over and sat at the end of one of the benches.

A hand fell on her shoulder and she turned to see Henry smiling at her. "Aren't you going to come sit down and eat?"

She peeked around at the men who had all sat at the table and appeared to be waiting for her to sit before dishing up. "Oh, I'm sorry. I wasn't sure..."

Harris came over and led her to the table while Henry went and sat in the large chair at the far end.

"Men, I'd like to introduce you to my wife, Patience. I expect her to be treated with the highest respect and if I ever catch anyone treating her with less, you will be gone. Do I make myself clear?" He held his stare on Dirk.

She could feel her cheeks burn as the men looked at her. Henry was watching it all with a wide smile on his face, giving her a subtle wink.

Harris introduced them by name but she wasn't sure she'd ever remember them all. She was too focused on how it felt to have a man treat her with respect and demand that others do the same.

In all her life she'd never known anything like it.

He then introduced her brother and told them he'd be helping around the ranch, so they were to show him the ropes.

She swallowed hard, then smiled at the men as

she moved to sit at the end of the bench beside her brother. Harris gently took her elbow and moved her to the other chair, pulling it out for her.

"This is where the lady of the house will sit."

She felt lightheaded as he pushed her back in, then went to sit in the place beside her.

As the men all started to fill her plates, she fought the tears that were threatening to fall. She met Harris's gaze and he nodded to her. "Make sure you get your own plate filled up. You look like you could use a good meal or two."

The men all started talking loudly, drowning out any reply she might have had. She watched as Harris dipped the spoon back into the bowl. He made sure Mark had another heaping portion of stew on his plate after he'd taken the small amount they normally would have been given.

"You're going to need more than that, young man. We've got a lot of work to do today."

Mark looked at her with eyes so wide she could see the whites against the paleness of his skin.

Never in her life could she remember feeling happiness like she did at this moment.

CHAPTER 9

"Seems they've taken a liking to you." Harris smiled down as he patted the blind dog behind the ears. "This fellow's name is Buster and wherever he is, you'll find Junior here not too far behind." The goat that was missing it's one hind leg, hopped over to be petted too.

He looked up and grinned when he saw the looks on Patience and Mark's faces as they looked down at the pair of animals. They'd met them briefly yesterday when they'd arrived but Mark had been in such a foul mood, they'd quickly walked into the house where he'd spent the remainder of the evening. It hadn't given them the chance to meet the animals on the ranch.

Now though, both animals were over rubbing against his legs. He was glad to see the boy smiling as he reached down to pet the goat that had perched beside him.

"Why is he called Junior?" Harris was surprised the boy was actually speaking to him.

"Well, from what I hear, when he came along he was a bit of a stubborn old goat. Elijah thought it'd be funny to name him after his friend, so his real name is actually Henry Junior. But we all call him Junior for short.

"Buster had arrived not too long before, his owners having left him behind because they figured he was no use to them. He'd pretty much given up until Junior arrived and became his eyes. They formed a bond and have been together just about every minute since."

Mark was now petting Buster, while Patience rubbed her hand along Junior's head. "That's so sad that someone would just leave an animal behind because he couldn't see." She lifted her eyes and met his. "What happened to Junior?" Her voice sounded so sad as she spoke about the animals.

"They said he'd been caught in a trap when Elijah came across him on one of the neighboring farms. The man was going to just shoot him but Elijah had paid for the goat and both he and Henry worked to save him by amputating his leg. Apparently, there wasn't anything the old man couldn't do and that included doing what he had to do to save an animal's life." He shook his head as he always did when speaking of the unbelievable things Elijah Chance had been able to do in his life.

"He sure sounds like an amazing man. I would have loved to meet him." Patience walked over closer to him. "I will admit, I was a bit shocked yesterday when we arrived and saw some of the animals but, I suspect, if I'd known Elijah, I wouldn't have been surprised at all."

He starting walking, motioning for them to follow. "He started his ranch with the usual cattle and horses you'd expect to find on a ranch. This spread still has just about one the largest herds in Kansas and makes most of the money from regular ranching. But it wasn't enough for Elijah. Any animal in need or without a home, found one here. He couldn't turn any away."

He knew he should be out working with the men and making them see that he was still prepared to do his share. Elijah had left big shoes to fill but thanks to Henry backing him this morning, he didn't expect too much trouble from most of them.

But he wanted Patience to settle in well on the ranch. He knew it was a lot to take in and he needed to make sure she was comfortable. She still had to stay for the entire six months for him to be able to win. And he knew this ranch was far from ordinary. It would take a special substance to be willing to commit to living out here with some of the animals making their homes here.

He looked over at her and noticed the color in her cheeks as she walked in the crisp air. Mark trailed behind, waiting so Buster and Junior could follow along.

Patience was looking all around, her smile covering her face as her eyes fell on the sights around her. She looked like a different woman today after getting a good night's rest and putting on one of the new skirts and blouses he'd gotten for her. When she'd stepped off the train, he'd noticed her beauty but today it was even more obvious.

He was glad he was able to be responsible, even if it was in a small way, for the smile on her face. Somehow he didn't think they'd had much to smile about in their lives.

"And this is Annie." He laughed at the expression on her face when she spotted the camel standing on the far side of the pen.

"So I did truly see this yesterday?" Her voice trailed off as she slowly turned her eyes to his.

"Yes, it's a camel. The army spent a great deal of money bringing in camels to act as beasts of burden, carrying supplies to forts down in Texas. Some of the herds ended up being split and used for various tasks, then eventually over the years, were sold off at auctions. Elijah had been at one such auction and saw Annie here. She was quite a scruffy looking soul at the time and no one was bidding on her. She was set to be disposed of after the auction but he went over and paid top price for her. He said she deserved to live out the rest of her days in luxury."

They kept walking and he showed her a few of the other animals, including a baby wolf whose mother had been killed, an ostrich, a badger, an armadillo, a buffalo, and an antelope. He was surprised that Patience never ran away scared or even seemed intimidated by any of the animals, especially since she'd grown up living in a town the size of Portland.

Instead, she'd reach her hand out and try to let any of them willing to come near enough have a sniff or a pat on the head.

"We have a lot of people who drive out here for tours and to see the animals, some of which they may never see otherwise. It's become quite a well-known ranch for sightseeing."

He felt a pride when he spoke about the ranch and he wasn't sure it was well earned. It wasn't like he'd started it himself, or done much of the work, but he was determined he would keep it going the way the old man had started it.

Mark had wandered off to get a better look at the animals, leaving him standing with Patience. He watched the boy walk away, with Buster and Junior following right behind. He knew he should take this chance to talk to Patience about everything but, for some reason, he felt a knot in his stomach when he thought about it.

But this was the plan he'd always had. He couldn't have second thoughts. Just because he'd expected to be saddled with a woman he'd never be able to tolerate spending time with and Patience had already proven she wasn't anything like that, he couldn't change his mind.

Could he?

and many tall...
...day is school day for you... about you...
expect the would... can you... to do her
life... coming more... and Tammy
had decided... behaved signing her... the
possible... kept...
what...

CHAPTER 10

M ark had gone off to his room, a smile on his face for the first time in as long as she could remember. He'd spent the evening talking about everything Harris had shown him today and then telling her how he'd gotten to help on the ranch. Most of the men seemed to have taken him under their wings too and made him feel welcome, taking the time to teach him the things he needed to learn.

She was sitting in a chair outside on the porch, unsure what to do with herself. Normally she would have had mending to do, dishes to clean or some other task that would keep her busy until she went to sleep.

Harris still hadn't come in for the night, so she was hoping to stay up until he did. She wanted the chance to talk about what he expected from the marriage. Everything felt like it had been so rushed and they hadn't really had much time alone since she'd arrived.

She tucked some of the loose strands of hair behind her ear, wishing her hair had been the same beautiful color as the woman they'd met at the train station. Her locks had been the color of butter and didn't seem to have a stray piece out of place.

Daniel had often told her how mousy her own hair was and had repeatedly told her to keep it up tighter so it didn't look so messy.

However, no matter how hard she tried, it just seemed to have a mind of its own.

She'd immediately noticed how strong and rugged Harrison had looked when she stepped off the train and she could have wept with joy to see he didn't seem to be the kind of man who would treat her unkindly.

She felt bad that he'd been so obviously disappointed and he'd even commented that she wasn't what he'd been expecting. She should have been more honest in her letter back to him but, at the time, all she could think about was getting away.

At least he'd been friendly and had made her feel welcome, even if she was left trying to figure out what her place would be here.

She closed her eyes and let the sounds of the night calm her worries. Never in her life had she heard such peaceful sounds. It was so quiet, she

could even make out the sound of the creek trick-
ling by at the back of the house. There was no
yelling from the saloon up the street, no sounds of
men fighting, only the quiet sounds of the animals
around the ranch as they settled in for the night.

"You didn't have to wait up for me. Sometimes I
can be out until late finishing up the chores around
here." She jumped as his voice broke through the
darkness.

"I wasn't ready to sleep, so thought I'd just have
some fresh air. It truly is beautiful here, Harris." She
felt her pulse quicken as he came up the steps and
sat in the chair beside her. With the glow of the
lantern beside him, she saw him look out at the
buildings scattered around the property.

"Yes, it is. I hope I can keep it running the way
Elijah had planned." He leaned forward and placed
his elbows on his knees. "I'm not sure I'm the best
man for the job but I'll do my best."

"Oh, I'm sure he wouldn't have left it for you if
he hadn't believed you were up to the job, Harris."
She couldn't understand why he would even think
such a thing. From what she'd seen, he was doing a
good job of looking after this ranch.

She knew it must have been a recent inheritance
since he'd only moved his own belongings into the
main house from the bunkhouse the same night she
and Mark had arrived.

But she also figured he'd talk to her about it when he was ready.

They sat in silence for a while, both listening to the sounds of the night around them.

"I know I wasn't quite what you were expecting when you sent for a bride and I'm sorry you were disappointed..." Her heart was in her throat as she said her worries out loud.

His head snapped around to look at her, his eyebrows furrowed deeply. "Why would you say that? I'm not disappointed. Truth is, I wasn't sure what to expect."

"Well, I know I must have looked a fright getting off the train in that old dress and I hadn't had much time to sleep along the way or to brush my hair for that matter. And then you said I wasn't quite what you'd expected so I thought perhaps you'd been..." She shrugged, unsure how to finish.

He smiled at her. Somehow, his smile always made her heart miss a beat. "That's what you thought?" He gave a little laugh as he shook his head.

"That wasn't what I meant. I'd had visions of ending up with an old hag who'd make my life a living hell. I wasn't disappointed to see you, in fact, I was pleasantly surprised."

He'd been happy to see her? Something about that statement made her entire body heat up.

"Oh, it's just that since I got here, I wasn't really sure..."

Harris turned and looked at her and his eyes caught hers in the glowing light. Her heart stuck in her throat as she waited to see what he was going to say.

"Harris! Ginny is having a hard time foaling. We've been trying to help her but she's losing strength and we're worried she can't do it." Whatever he'd been about to tell her got interrupted when one of the men ran over from the barn.

She stood up too, running into the back of him as he stopped on the stairs and turned around. "Where do you think you're going?"

She stepped back and looked up at him. "To help you. I've helped bring more than my fair share of foals into this world working at the stables, so I'm not just going to let the horse suffer when I know I can help."

She brushed past him and down the stairs behind the man who was standing, grinning at her, ignoring the confused look on Harris's face.

Just because she didn't know what her role was here, it didn't mean she'd just sit around and do nothing.

CHAPTER 11

H arris turned his head slightly, not wanting anyone to see him watching her. What was the matter with him? She was his wife after all, so it isn't like anyone would think anything much about it.

It was himself who was feeling confused. He'd had his fair share of women clinging to him over the years, especially the months he'd spent drifting from town to town searching for what he was missing in his life.

He'd never had any problem catching a woman's eye and as soon as he mentioned his famous last name, they'd soon be declaring their undying love.

But none of those women had ever caught his eye or his heart. There hadn't been anything to make any of them stand apart and, in fact, they were all the same shallow people who treated him differently because of his name.

He laughed to himself as he wondered what all of those "ladies" would think if they knew about some of the things he'd done in his life? Although, he was sure if they still believed they were going to get some financial gain from him, it wouldn't matter.

Patience was different and he'd noticed it from the first time he saw her. There was a goodness, a kindness in her, that he'd never seen in anyone in his life. She was the kind of woman who deserved to be treated like a queen yet didn't ask for anything.

He couldn't understand what he was feeling toward her and it had him rattled. There was nothing that made her stand out as far as her beauty but she had something that drew his eyes. Her eyes could hold him in one spot without saying a word. And he knew she hated her hair but after she'd taken her bonnet off that first day, he hadn't been able to take his eyes off it.

She'd only been here a few days yet he was finding himself thinking maybe he'd like her to stay and see what could happen between them.

But he was also starting to think maybe she deserved someone who could offer her marriage for the right reasons and not a man who had questionable morals at the best of times.

"Harris, come here and help me. I have to give

her a hand. It's coming out backward and poor mama here just doesn't have any more strength." He'd seen Elijah help with a birth like this one time and he knew it hadn't been easy. However, Patience seemed so calm and sure of what she was about to do, he honestly believed she could pull it off.

"Run and grab, Henry. Tell him to come and give us a hand." Harris stood to move closer to Patience and help, while the other man set off to ride over to Henry's.

They were left alone, standing so close Harris was sure he could feel her breath on his cheek as he bent over to help. He watched in amazement as she started to maneuver the foal. The back end was the first to be born just as she'd predicted.

"Here, you need to help me pull down a bit to help her. The cord will likely already be broken now, so we need to help this along as quick as we can." He felt like a child, unsure where to touch or what to do but she indicated with her head where he needed to grab. She smiled at him as though she had no doubt he was going to be able to help her.

Together, they pulled on the foal, bringing it into the world when he caught its front legs in his arms. They were covered in substances that would leave most women hollering in disgust but when he looked at Patience, she was beaming as he gently laid the foal down beside the tired mother.

"You did it. I'm pretty sure they both would

have died if you hadn't known what to do." He noticed her cheeks turn red, even in the darkness of the barn only lit with the lantern hanging from a nail up above.

She sat back, letting the mother lick the new baby. "I had to help a few horses when I worked at the stables outside the boardinghouse. One time, I couldn't save either the mother or the foal. I paid dearly for that. So I made sure I did everything I could to save them from then on."

He watched her face fall as she remembered and didn't know what to say. He stood and reached his hand out to take hers and help her to her feet. They didn't say anything as he led her to the door of the stall and handed her a cloth to wipe her hands.

"Did they hurt you a lot, Patience?" His voice was low and his heart thundered in his chest as he imagined the small woman in front of him having to face the beatings he was sure she endured.

She kept her eyes on her hands as she wiped them clean, then handed him the cloth, still not meeting his eyes. She gave a small shrug. "It wasn't so bad the past few years. Mark always stepped in. But when he was smaller, they needed someone to take it out on and I guess I was their choice."

He set the cloth back on the stall and found his fingers reaching out to touch her cheek.

"If I ever see either of them, they're going to answer to me." His voice sounded rough in his ears.

It bothered him more than he could understand to think about them ever hitting her.

She lifted her head and met his eyes, then she smiled. "Well, I hope we never see either of them again."

They stood looking at each other with the sounds of the foal whickering in the stall as the mother licked it clean. His fingers softly caressed her cheek, barely moving.

"What happened? Did she manage all right?" Henry's worried voice slammed into the quiet around them and Harris pulled his hand back like he'd been burned.

He kept his eyes on her face, though, and he suddenly wished he could make everyone else disappear. What was happening to him?

He was sure he must just be feeling bad about the life she had lived and like he needed to make it up to her somehow. She was a bit like one of the wounded animals who'd found their way here and he wanted to give her the chance for some happiness.

But at what cost would it come to him?

He worried that now, it might cost him more than he'd bargained for.

CHAPTER 12

The small building was packed full but as Patience looked around, there were only a few other women besides herself. Harris had mentioned there weren't many other women in Romance but somehow she'd believed there would be more than she was seeing here today.

While Henry spoke, she let herself peek over at her husband sitting beside her. It still felt strange to admit to herself that she was someone's wife, especially since they weren't married in the sense she'd always imagined to be.

Even though he'd always been kind to her, since the night in the barn, he seemed to be more interested in spending time with her. She didn't know what to make of her relationship with Harris but she was so thankful to be here with him, she didn't want to risk anything by asking him.

She looked down at his hands, resting on his knees. She smiled to herself as she remembered those fingers gently touching her cheek. She'd been sure he was going to kiss her but Henry had come in to check on the horse and interrupted. Since then, they hadn't had the chance to be alone, so she didn't know if he really would have or not.

He was now drumming his fingers impatiently as Henry continued to talk. She lifted her eyes and caught him watching her. He winked, then gave her a smile that made her breath catch in her throat. Quickly averting her eyes, she felt her cheeks start to burn knowing he'd seen her looking at him.

Thankfully, Henry finished his service and everyone stood to head back outside. As she took her turn to step into the aisle, Harris lightly touched his hand to her back to help her. Instantly, she felt her skin tingle beneath her dress. How could he have this effect on her? Surely, it was just because she hadn't had the opportunity to be around many men in her life besides the ones who stayed at the boardinghouse and treated her like a servant.

He kept his hand on her back as they made their way into the fresh air and walked down the steps. The church was one of the few buildings in town. Henry had insisted it had to be one of the first ones constructed when he and Elijah had first arrived in the area.

Henry had ridden with them since Harris had opted to bring the wagon. Now, they stood at the wagon waiting for Henry to finish talking to the townsfolk as they left the church.

Mark jumped up into the back of the wagon and Patience smiled at how much happier he looked already. They'd been here a few days now and the change in him was unbelievable. He looked forward to going out and helping the men with the ranch and, no matter where he went, Buster and Junior were under his feet.

He had a purpose and he was even beginning to look stronger and healthier with the good food he had to eat and the home he now felt he had.

Harris put his hand out for her to take so he could help her up into the wagon. As she turned, he was standing closer than she realized and she ended up being pressed right up against his chest.

"Oh, I'm sorry. I didn't mean to bump you." Once again, her cheeks immediately burned as she tried to step back.

"That's all right. I could think of worse things to have happen." Harris was grinning at her, not letting her move back as he still held her hand firmly in his.

They stood staring at each other while she could hear people milling around outside the church. Her heart was beating so loud she could hear it and she worried everyone around them could too.

"Since the day is so nice, I thought it'd be a good

day to invite everyone out for a day on the ranch. We can lay out some blankets, set out some food and enjoy one of the last warm days of the season." Harris rolled his eyes as Henry's voice once again interrupted them.

Harris turned his head and raised an eyebrow in Henry's direction. "So now we have to go home and prepare a feast for the entire town of Romance?"

Henry chuckled. "Well, since half of them already work or live on the ranch and would have been eating there anyway and the rest of the people have offered to bring their own offerings, I think we can manage." Henry turned to smile at Patience.

"While I have no doubt you're more than capable of handling it all on your own, I'd be happy to help you with anything you need to get things ready."

She had to smile back at the older man. "Well, we better get back and get to work." The fact that Harris was still holding her hand, with her pressed up close to him, was rattling her. So the sooner she could get sitting in the wagon and away from the warmth of his body, the better she'd be able to think.

As she turned to step up, his hands went to her waist, and she felt her step falter again. She knew she really needed to pull herself together and stop letting herself get so flustered when she was around him.

She moved to the center of the seat, making room for Henry to climb up behind her. Harris went around and climbed up on the other side, and she was sure he'd moved as far in her direction as he could.

Making their way out of town, she tried to keep her senses under control while her leg bumped into his and her whole body kept crashing against his with every bounce of the wagon.

The men all talked around her, even Mark who seemed excited for the event taking place at the ranch. Being around men who treated him kindly, and as an equal, was doing so much for his confidence. He was happily sharing ideas for everything they could do today.

She couldn't say a word as she sat caught in a haze of confusion about what she was feeling. Being this close to Harris was creating a jumble of feelings she couldn't understand. It wasn't like he'd mentioned anything about making their marriage more than it was and she still wondered if maybe she'd still be sent away after the six months she was required to stay.

But something had changed for her. She was finding herself thinking about Harris all the time and when she was around him, she couldn't seem to think straight.

She knew she wasn't as beautiful as Jane, the woman Dirk had brought with him to church today.

She lacked the refinement the other woman had demonstrated today. Patience had watched Jane holding her hands out for men to kiss, while she looked down demurely and gave a small curtsy to each one.

Patience had felt dull next to the radiance Jane had brought to the small church. The men had all been clamoring to be introduced, while Dirk had stood proudly beside her.

She felt bad, wondering what Harris had been thinking having her on his arm. Seeing the ranch in the distance, she let her eyes peek up to catch a glimpse of the man beside her before the crowd arrived.

This time her heart did stop beating for a moment when she caught his eyes smiling down at her.

She was beginning to think he might be bad for her health.

CHAPTER 13

He watched as she set the pie down on the table he'd carried outside with one of the men. She smiled at the people who were gathered around and introduced herself to anyone she didn't know.

He felt bad, knowing there were only about three other women in Romance who would be here today but he had no doubt she'd make friends with them in record time.

Of course, Jane would be here too. She'd been staying at the small boardinghouse in town since she arrived. He knew Dirk had gone to town a few times to see her and he assumed she was sticking around in case Patience didn't stay for the six months. Then, Dirk could marry her and win the ranch.

Harris didn't know why Dirk didn't just go

ahead and marry the woman anyway. It wasn't like women were abundant in these parts and even though she wasn't the type of woman he'd want to be stuck with for life, she seemed suited to Dirk.

He'd noticed Patience watching Jane today as she flitted from man to man, introducing herself and batting her eyelashes at them all. His heart had clenched when he saw her reach down and wipe at her skirts self-consciously, knowing she didn't feel like she measured up.

There was a time he'd have likely been over there with those men, fawning all over the new beauty in town, knowing he'd win her over with a simple smile in her direction.

But his eyes had only been able to see Patience today. Where Jane had a striking beauty that was visible to the eye, it was also obvious that her beauty didn't go any further. It was evident in how she spoke to others and how she treated them.

Whereas Patience had a beauty that shone through brighter than anything a woman like Jane could ever hope to have. When she smiled, it was like everything around her stopped moving and she was only looking at the person she was speaking to.

In all his life, he'd never found himself drawn to a woman so different from all the others he'd met.

"Might want to stop staring with your mouth hanging open or the men around here'll start thinking your smitten with your new wife." Henry came up behind him, slapping him hard on the shoulder.

"Henry, why must you always sneak up on people?"

"Well, I wasn't really sneakin' if you'd been paying attention. I called your name a couple times and you didn't answer me."

He scowled in Henry's direction. "Is there something I can help you with?"

"Just thought you should know that Dirk's been spouting off that there's no way you'll be able to stay married to a plain Jane like Patience and that he'll win this ranch yet. The other men aren't paying him much mind. Partly because I think all of the men working on this ranch have become quite fond of Patience, so don't really put much weight to what the man says."

Harris looked back at Patience, the woman Dirk said was plain, and felt his heart lurch when she lifted her head and smiled at him. He was almost sure he saw her cheeks go red before she put her head back down to set the pieces of pie on the plates in front of her.

There was nothing plain about her. She wore a bonnet on her head but the hair peeking out framed her face and shone in the sunlight. The eyes that had first met his on the train platform were the color of the sky on a clear day. He'd never seen a smile like the one she wore on her face every day.

And yet, she was the one person who'd likely never had a reason to smile.

"Dirk can say what he wants. Patience won't be going anywhere." He'd already decided when he got the chance to be alone with her again, he'd like to talk to her about the possibility of making their marriage more than in name only.

Which meant she hopefully wouldn't be leaving after the six months were up. He knew he'd still never really explained it all to her and she hadn't been the type to harp on him and demand answers.

She was just happy to be here and see her brother safe.

His teeth clenched together at the same time he heard Henry groan. He'd obviously been watching Patience too and noticed when Dirk had walked over to the table with Jane in tow.

They both knew Dirk wouldn't be going over to make small talk with her.

"Would you like a piece of pie, Dirk?" She smiled at the man in front of her, then turned to look at Jane. "Your dress is beautiful, Jane. The color really suits you."

Dirk had taken the pie from her hand and was standing watching her with a smirk on his face.

Harris walked right up so he was standing beside Patience, making sure Dirk knew he was there.

"This old thing? Well, it's all right. I don't want to wear my good dresses out here. They'd likely just get ruined anyway." Harris saw Patience's smile falter a bit.

"Nice to see you bought your wife some more sturdy dresses than that sack she was wearing when she arrived in town." Dirk laughed around a mouthful of pie.

"Dirk, if you are just over here wanting to cause trouble, move on. This day was for the townsfolk to have some fun together and it's been a wonderful day so far. We don't need you stirring things up." Henry's voice spoke from behind him.

Dirk shoveled the last bite of pie into his mouth and set the plate down, then raised his hands as though, he was surrendering.

"I'm not trying to cause any trouble. Just thought Patience might like to meet another woman to talk to, since she's stuck out here on this ranch with nothing but a bunch of dusty ranch hands every day."

Harris gritted his teeth, knowing full well that wasn't all Dirk was here to do. He was going to try causing trouble, Harris had no doubt about that.

Jane offered Harris one of her dazzling smiles, sure it would soften him up. But she spoke her words to Patience, "You're a lucky girl, Patience. Showing up just in the nick of time to get Harris married so he could inherit this ranch and the fortune that goes with it. I'm pretty certain, at that point, he'd have married just about anyone who came along. Now he's got the ranch and the money so after the six months is up, Harris can send you on your way and live the life of luxury he won."

He heard Patience softly set the knife she'd been holding to cut the pie onto the table. Jane winked at him. "You know, you didn't have to go through with marrying her. I was there. You could have married me. I'd have been more than willing and then you wouldn't be stuck trying to pretend you are happily married to her for the next six months." Jane turned and shook her head in Patience's direction as though she couldn't understand why he'd gone through with marrying the other woman.

This time, it was Dirk's turn to get angry. "What are you talking about? You agreed to come out here and marry me!"

But Harris wasn't listening to their argument anymore.

Patience had turned to face him and tears filled eyes that were large in her now pale face. He desperately wanted to reach out to her but he didn't know what he could say.

"If you all will excuse me, I'm going to go back to the house and get some more pies to bring out."

She walked away with her head held high but not before he saw the pain reflected on her face.

He turned back to Dirk. "You can get your things and clear out. You're no longer welcome on this ranch."

"You can't fire me! You haven't been given full rights to this ranch yet, so I'm not going anywhere." Dirk was grabbing Jane by the arm, prepared to drag her away to finish their argument.

"He might not have the authority but I do. Now do as he says and clear your things out. I don't want to see you this side of the fence again."

Henry strode over and took Dirk by the elbow, making sure he made his way to the bunk house immediately.

Harris turned and watched Patience enter the house. He knew he was going to have to fix the damage the words caused today but he didn't know where to start.

CHAPTER 14

She pulled her legs up tight and tucked them beneath her skirt, leaning her chin on her knees as she wrapped her arms around them. The creek trickled by softly and she let the soothing sound calm her heart as she watched it work its way over the rocks that were determined to stop it from flowing past.

She felt a lot like the water, plain and ordinary, with nothing really dazzling to offer the world. And everywhere she went, it seemed there were stones and obstacles that tried to slow her down and stop her.

A wet nose reached around and touched her cheek, followed by a tongue that licked a tear away. Smiling, she turned her head to give Buster a pat on the head. Of course, Junior was right beside him, demanding she give him some attention, too.

Her brother walked over and sat beside her, not saying anything. She'd known as soon as she saw the animals, Mark wouldn't be far behind.

"You all right, Patience?" His voice seemed to have grown deeper since they arrived.

She offered him a weak smile. "I'm fine. Just needed some time to myself. It's been such a hard week, leaving the Thompson's, moving here and then getting married. It's a lot to take in." Buster was nudging her with his nose, trying to lie down and wanting to put his head on her lap.

Mark didn't say anything as he picked up a rock and threw it at the water. They both watched as it skipped across on top before sinking.

"What did Dirk and that woman say to you?"

Her stomach somersaulted as she realized he must have seen the exchange. She didn't think anyone else had noticed but had been embarrassed enough that Harris and Henry had been there to see it.

She shrugged. "Nothing really. They just pointed out that perhaps Harris was stuck with me and would have married anyone when I arrived. Apparently, he needed me to marry him so quickly because it was part of a wager the men out here were all hoping to win. The prize was the deed to this ranch and the fortune that the man who built it left in his will."

Mark went silent again, so she turned her eyes

to look at him. He was clenching his jaw tightly and she could see the muscles moving as he ground his teeth together.

"Mark, we knew it was something out of the ordinary for him to be advertising for a bride so quickly without corresponding first. And we knew he'd said I was only obligated to stay for six months. Apparently, that's part of the stipulations." She looked down at the dog whose ears she was scratching while he slept on her lap.

"It's not like he lied to me." Her words didn't come out as strong as she'd hoped they would.

The truth was, she was hurt and she didn't even understand why.

She'd been humiliated when Jane had said those things and even when Dirk had mentioned about Harris needing to buy her a dress. But these were all things she'd always known. She couldn't pretend she was more than she was.

But why hadn't Harris just told her everything from the beginning? It's not like she had anywhere else to go. She would have still married him but she might have been able to stop herself from believing something more might be possible over time.

All she was to him was a way to get his fortune. It had nothing to do with her at all and she'd been a fool to even start thinking there was a chance for it to be otherwise.

Now she felt like a fool. She'd managed to get

through the rest of the day without embarrassing herself further, then helped get everything cleaned up. Harris had tried to talk to her numerous times but she made sure she always had something to do or someone around to avoid it.

She wasn't ready to face him.

Patience was confused and didn't know why she felt so hurt. A week ago, she hadn't even met him but already she'd found herself thinking there was a possibility for a future here for her.

Today, she realized how naive she'd been.

As soon as everyone had left and the men headed out to do the chores, she'd snuck down here to be alone.

"Mark, can I talk to your sister for a minute?"

Harris's voice crashed into her thoughts. Her head flew up to see him standing behind Mark, looking down at her. Even Buster lifted his head, startled at the intrusion into his sleep.

Mark turned to look at her with a question in his eyes. She knew he'd stay and protect her like he always had if he thought she needed it. But she just nodded her head at him, knowing she couldn't avoid Harris for much longer anyway.

Mark stood and as soon as he did, Junior moved over to push his nose at Buster, telling him it was time to get up and come with him. She watched the three of them walk away but not before Mark was sure to give Harris a stare that let him know he didn't appreciate seeing his sister cry.

She turned back and let her fingers play with a seam on her dress as the sound of the water wound between them.

"Mind if I sit down?"

"Of course you can, Harris. It's your land." She didn't really mean to sound so biting and she inwardly cringed as she spoke the words out loud.

She kept her eyes on the creek, watching as a bird flitted along the opposite bank trying to find bugs to eat. Her heart thumped in her chest, worried about what Harris would have to say to her.

Even though she was upset about everything she'd learned today, she knew he'd never lied to her. And the truth was, she didn't want to go anywhere.

She'd like to stay here as long as he'd let her. Even if it meant losing her heart.

Patience loved the feeling of peacefulness here and she was happy to see the smile on her brother's face. She couldn't take that from him. Not until they'd had more time to heal.

Now though, as she waited for him to speak, with her heart in her throat, she suddenly realized she could be about to lose everything.

CHAPTER 15

He sat staring across at the same birds she was watching. The air was cool around them as the last days of fall settled in. He glanced over and saw she'd only wore a light shawl when she came down here. The evenings got cold quickly as the sun went down so she was likely wishing she'd worn something warmer.

He realized then, she probably didn't have anything warmer. That was something he was going to be sure he remedied the next time they went to Abilene.

Shrugging out of the heavy duster he wore, he wrapped it around her shoulders. Her fingers brushed his as she pulled it tight around her chest. She smiled up at him but it wasn't reflected in her eyes.

"Thank you. It's quite a bit chillier now than when I first walked down here."

They sat in silence a moment as he struggled to find the words he wanted to say. What had happened to him?

A week ago he'd been a completely sane man and now, thanks to a woman, he was having trouble thinking straight.

"Patience, what Jane said wasn't all true, I hope you know that." May as well just jump in with both boots.

"It's fine, Harris. You don't need to explain to me. I knew the terms of the marriage were different. You never lied to me." She smiled up at him again. "It wasn't like I expected anything more anyway."

Why did her smile wrench his heart so tightly?

"No, Patience, I owe you an explanation. I should have told you everything right from the beginning but I hadn't ever really expected things to become so complicated. I was going to tell you as soon as you arrived but for some reason, I just couldn't bring myself to explain it to you. Then after you were here a few days, I found myself enjoying being around you and I was happy to see the smile on your face. I guess I didn't want to let you down. I can tell your life may not have been easy up 'till now..."

"So you felt sorry for me?" She interrupted and this time when she looked at him, her eyes flashed anger in them.

He was making a mess of this explanation.

"No, Patience. Just let me talk. I'm not good with explaining myself." He pushed his hand through his hair in frustration. His hat fell to the back, so he pulled it forward again as he tried to figure out how to word what he was trying to say.

He looked at her sideways. "You've likely heard the Winchester name?"

She gave a slight shrug as she nodded.

"Everyone has."

"Well, you may have wondered if I was part of those Winchesters." She didn't say anything, just kept her eyes on his.

"I am. But not in the immediate family. I was given the option to work in the business if I wanted but it would never be mine. I would never be much more than a paid worker. Any ideas or plans I had weren't important. But that didn't matter. When you have a name like Winchester, people treat you different. Women threw themselves at me without knowing anything about me. Once they found out I wasn't high enough on the family ladder, they'd move on. I needed to find my own place, away from the Winchester name."

He swallowed, not sure why he'd thought he had

to explain everything from his past but he figured he may as well continue. His knees were pulled up in front of him and he rested his elbows on them as he looked out over the field in the distance.

"I started making my way west, unsure what I was even going to do. Along the way, I made some bad decisions in my quest to make my own fortune. I guess I was angry about being shackled to a name that wouldn't ever do me any good anyway. I gambled, I cheated, and I lied to get what I wanted. There were some good people who I wish I could go back and give the money I won from them by knowing how to cheat at the tables."

He was scared to look at her now, afraid he'd see disgust in her eyes.

"I'd lost who I was until one day when I cheated a man who'd bet his farm. When I saw the look on his face, and knowing I'd cheated, I hated who I'd become. I couldn't take everything from a man who'd gambled everything, hoping to win enough money to put food on his family's table. I walked away, letting him keep the farm and hopped on my horse. I haven't sat at a table since and I decided then I would do what I had to do to make my own way honestly."

He turned his head to see her reaction to what he'd told her. She was just staring ahead, so he took the moment to let his eyes take her all in. Her cheeks were red from the cool air that was blowing on them and her skin was flawless. Even though they weren't looking at him, he could see the bright blue color of her eyes.

Her hair was hanging down her shoulders, having long ago come loose from the bun she'd tied it in this morning. The brown tendrils that hung around her face called to him, begging him to reach out and wrap them around his fingers.

"I'd taken this job on the ranch hoping to earn my way honestly. And to learn from Elijah Chance. The ranch seemed like it was my own last chance and I wanted to make it my opportunity to learn and maybe start my own place someday. When he died, and had that clause in his will, I had to try."

His fingers finally found their way over. He couldn't resist and as he felt the softness of her hair, she turned to look at him. His heart leaped from his chest as he peered into the blue depths.

"It was only meant to be a business arrangement with the woman who would agree to come out here. I figured I'd hate her and she'd be easy enough to convince to stay with the offer of paying her dearly at the end of the six months. Then she could then be off on her way and we'd both continue on with our lives. I never thought it would be more than that."

She wasn't saying anything, just staring at him.

"But when you stepped off the train and smiled at me, I felt the guilt and shame of what I'd done before. I'd messed with someone else's future with only concern for my own. I just couldn't bring myself to explain the whole arrangement to you."

"I would have still married you, Harris. I didn't have anywhere else to go and I knew as soon as I saw you, you wouldn't hurt us. I knew you'd be kind."

His heart plummeted. "That's what I mean. What kind of man gambles with someone else's future? I don't deserve to win the ranch if it means I've hurt someone along the way. And somehow, since you came here, I realized the original plan I had for a business arrangement might not be the one I truly wanted anymore."

She furrowed her brows together. "What do you mean?"

"I mean, you've got me confused, Patience. Until now, I've never thought of anything more in my future other than earning money and making my own fortune. I was consumed with it. I'd never really thought about settling down but, lately, I'm not so sure."

Her throat moved as she swallowed hard. Before he even knew what he was doing, he leaned toward her, sliding the hand that had been in her hair down to rest on her shoulder. Her eyes widened as his face moved closer and he could feel her breath warm on his lips.

Suddenly, a cry broke out on the other side of the creek behind some trees that lined the bank. He sat back quickly, moving his head toward the sound.

"What was that, Harris?" Patience's voice shook with fear and he hoped perhaps a bit of lingering emotion from the kiss they'd almost shared.

He was already standing up and he reached his hand out to help her up. "Stay here. I'm going to see."

The sound wasn't like anything he'd heard before. It was a combination of despair and agony but it wasn't an animal he was familiar with.

"Be careful!" The concern in her voice warmed his insides. It had been a long time since anyone had worried about him.

He crossed the shallow water and moved toward the sound that was now just low guttural sounds. As he pushed the branches back, he could see something lying in the darkness of the setting sun around them.

Reaching down, he released the trap that was clamped down on the leg. His jaw tightened at the thought of someone setting a trap on his property and now this poor animal was suffering.

Lifting the poor creature in his arms, he turned to carry it back to the house.

Patience's eyes met his and he saw the tears as she took in the sight of the injured baby fox.

Whispering to the animal in his arms, he made his way back across the water. "Don't worry, little fella, if anyone can help heal you, it's the woman standing right here."

CHAPTER 16

"Have you found any more traps lying around?" Patience could hear Harris talking to Henry on the other side of the pen. She was in checking on Tucker, as she'd affectionately named the little fox. The name had come from somewhere in her memories and she thought it would make a fine name for him.

He'd been in a bad way when they'd found him but he was starting to respond now to the care he'd been given over the past couple of weeks. The poor animal had, obviously, been lying there for a while and had been sorely dehydrated and hungry. His leg had ended up with an infection but she'd kept tending to the wound until it was finally starting to heal.

It looked like he was finally out of the woods and he'd become quite attached to Patience. Her heart broke for the animal knowing that after they'd brought him in and started tending to him, Harris and some of the other men had gone back out to see if they could find more traps. They'd found another fox that had been caught in a trap near that one and they'd realized it had been Tucker's mother. He'd been on his own after that, likely having watched his mother die before ending up in his own trap and it made her sick to the stomach knowing how much he'd suffered.

After a search around the property, a few more traps had been found but, thankfully, no more animals had been caught in them.

Harris had been furious. He'd been going over every square inch of the property making sure they found them all and the men had all been instructed to now keep their eyes peeled for any suspicious activity on the ranch. Whoever was setting them had no right to do so and he wanted them caught.

She stood up, wiping her skirts as she walked out of the pen. Harris turned and smiled as she walked toward them.

"How's he doing today?"

"He's good. I think his leg has healed and he's eating well on his own." She pulled the warm coat that Harris had brought her back from his trip to Abilene tight around her shoulders. She'd been so surprised when he came home with it. Even though he'd bought all those clothes for her and Mark when they'd arrived, she'd always felt like he'd done it out of obligation or a sense of duty for his new wife.

But this jacket was special to her because she'd never had anyone buy her something "just because." She could have made do with the sweater she had but he'd insisted she should have something warmer.

She looked toward Henry who was standing beside Harris. "Would you like to come in and have a cup of tea to warm up before you head home?" The wind was starting to pick up around them.

"No thanks, Patience. I have to head to my old shack and get things cleaned up a bit before my daughter and her husband come here for a few days. It's been a while since they've visited and I'm afraid this old man has let the place get a little dusty around the edges." She smiled as he winked at her. He was so excited that his daughter was coming for a visit and had been talking about it for days.

She left the men to discuss what they were going to do about the traps and finish up the last of the chores. Henry had said he could smell snow in the air, so they knew they'd need to get the animals all penned up warm and dry.

The season for visitors to the ranch was done, not many people wanted to come this way and wander around the grounds looking at the animals in the colder weather. She hoped she would still be here by next year when the ranch opened back up to visitors.

As she walked to the house, she let the wind blow her hair back while she took in the view around her. Even in the grips of winter starting around them, she could see the beauty of the land surrounding the ranch house. Some may say the ranch was in a desolate place in the middle of nowhere but she could see the beauty that she was sure had drawn Elijah here in the first place.

But even after a few weeks here, she wasn't sure where things were going. That day by the creek, she'd been sure Harris was going to kiss her and tell her he'd like her to stay. But they hadn't seemed to be able to find any time alone to finish the conversation.

Looking after Tucker had kept her busy while Harris and the rest of the ranch hands were busy cleaning up the ranch and preparing for winter with the animals. Then there'd been Dirk who'd been causing a ruckus in town, claiming he'd been unfairly fired and Harris would pay once he ended up winning the ranch from him.

The wind blew in the door behind her and she shivered before she pulled off her jacket, letting the heat from the fire she'd stoked before going outside warm her up. She moved to the stove to put the kettle on, knowing both Harris and Mark would appreciate a hot drink when they came in.

She let her mind wander as she stood with her arms crossed in front of her by the heat of the stove, forcing the chill out of her body.

She'd formed a quiet bond with Harris and she thought he seemed to enjoy being around her. They spent a great deal of time talking when they had the chance and she'd learned a lot about him in the days she'd been here. She could see he was a good man who'd made some bad choices that he still carried the guilt for.

But he was determined to make his future something he could be proud of and she'd found herself hoping, beyond reason, that future would include her. She'd never had the experience to be around men like this, so she was unsure how to let him know she'd like to stay. It didn't seem the proper thing to do.

Lost in her thoughts, she jumped when Harris walked up beside her.

"Harris, you startled me! I didn't even hear you come through the door."

He was grinning, something she'd found always disarmed her. His smile had a way of rendering her almost speechless.

"I noticed. I came through the door like a stampeding herd of buffalo and you didn't even flinch." His scent reached her nose as he put his hands out to warm them closer to the stove. A mixture of cool air and leather combined to give him a purely masculine scent that caused her stomach to do a flip.

She turned to grab him a cup to make some tea but he reached out and took hold of her hand first. He reached down and lifted her other hand into his. He was smiling at her and, instantly, her heart started racing. Her cheeks were burning, uncomfortable at the closeness in the warmth of the room and him standing so close to her.

"We haven't had much time to be alone together in the past few days. It seems like there's always something or someone interrupting."

She swallowed, trying to ease the dryness she suddenly felt in her throat. His thumb was caressing the back of her hand and she was sure he could hear the pounding of her heart against her chest in the quiet of the room.

As though on cue, the front door was flung open and the snow that had finally started to fall, swirled into the room. Harris cursed loudly as he dropped one of her hands and spun around to see who had interrupted this time.

Henry was standing there with a white haze of cold and snow falling around him. "Harris, we have a problem. Annie is missing. The gate to her pen is open and she got away before the snow fell, so we don't even have any tracks to follow."

"What do you mean she's missing? I told Mark to bed her down for the night a few hours ago."

Harris had dropped her other hand and was already walking over to take his still cold jacket off the hook.

"That's what I thought but I went to do a final check around the pens before I headed home. That's when I saw the open gate."

Harris looked at her. "Where's Mark?" She was surprised at how fast his voice had gone from kind and tender to the anger he was barely controlling now.

"I don't know. I haven't seen him." She was already heading toward his room. She hadn't seen him come in but maybe he was already in there. Going in his room, she searched around for clues to see where he could have gone.

As she was about to go back out to tell Harris he wasn't here, she spotted a piece of paper sitting on his bed. Her heart sank as she was overcome with dread.

Picking it up, her eyes filled with tears as she read the words. She ran back out to the main room.

"He's gone, Harris! He said he forgot to latch the gate and he knew you'd be mad."

Harris strode over and ripped the note from her hands. His eyes scanned the words as he shook his head. Crumpling it up, he threw it on the floor.

"Henry, get the others. You go find Annie and I'll go find Mark."

Patience ran to grab her coat from the hook but

before she could put it on, Harris took hold of her arm. "Where do you think you're going?"

"He's my brother. I'm going with you." She pulled her arm free from his grasp and put her coat on.

"No, Patience. I'm not letting you come out in this. You're staying here and I'm not listening to any argument. I can't be worrying about you out there too. Just stay put and I will find him."

She was fighting hard not to cry but as she looked at Harris, her tears started to spill over. Harris groaned softly and pulled her into his arms. His hand caressed the back of her hair as he held her.

"Harris, he's all I have. Please, find him," her voice shook with emotion as she let his arms comfort her.

Holding her tightly against his chest, she could feel it rumble as he spoke, "I promise I will find him, Patience. You have to trust me."

He pulled back and looked down into her eyes. All she could do was nod as he lifted his hand and wiped a tear with his thumb.

"Be careful." Her voice sounded strangled as she watched him turn and go out the door.

Letting her legs fold beneath her, she sat on the floor and wept. Her brother had been so afraid of being beaten again, he'd run away instead of just telling someone what he'd done.

And now, the only two men she cared about were out in a snowstorm and she sat here unable to do anything to help.

Suddenly remembering the words he'd said, she realized she did trust Harris. And she knew he wouldn't give up until he'd found her brother.

She just hoped he wasn't too late.

CHAPTER 17

The wind whipped around him as he struggled to see what was ahead. The snow was coming down in a constant sheet of white and even with the small lantern he held, he couldn't see more than a foot in front of him. Not wanting to risk injury to his horse, he kept her at a slow pace while he yelled Mark's name.

He couldn't tell how long he'd been out here and he couldn't even be sure how far he'd come. He racked his brain for places that Mark could have gone to hide out as he tried to get a hold of his fury over the boy running away.

Seeing the fear and desperation in Patience's eyes had torn the heart from his chest. He hated seeing her so upset and when she'd said Mark was all she had, he'd wanted so badly to let her know she would never be alone so long as he was breathing.

But it wasn't the time and he knew how much she loved her brother. For years, they'd only had each other and she'd grieve deeply if anything ever happened to him.

He wouldn't let that happen.

He had to admit that, even though he was angry at Mark. It wasn't because he'd left the gate open and Annie had escaped—he knew it would have been an accident. While he knew he'd have to let the boy know to be more careful, he didn't need to run away and hide from him.

He was angrier that he'd do something this foolish and scare his sister like this. And if he was being completely honest, he was a bit sore that once again he'd been interrupted as he tried to talk to Patience about the possibility of making their marriage permanent.

Every time he got up the courage to talk to her, something came up and got in the way. He wasn't sure why he was so nervous about talking to her like this. It wasn't like he hadn't had his share of luck with women over the years; in fact, he was quite used to having women throwing themselves at his feet. He'd never really had to be the one chasing a woman.

And what made it even more frustrating was that the woman he was chasing now was his own wife.

He pulled his jacket up around his neck as he

tugged down on his hat to keep it from blowing away in the wind. The sun had completely set now so he wasn't sure how he was going to find anything in the darkness with the wind blowing the snow all around him.

How was he going to tell Patience he couldn't find her brother? And that if he didn't find shelter over night, the chances wouldn't be good for him.

A noise in front of him had him squinting into the darkness to see if he'd imagined it or if it was real.

Once again, barking could be heard just in the distance. His stomach sunk as he noticed the rocky outcropping that meant the ravine was ahead. It wasn't a large drop but for someone unfamiliar with the land, it could easily become a hazard.

He moved his mare forward, following the sound of the barking while he held the lantern higher. Suddenly, he could make out the form of an animal rushing toward him.

Junior!

They hadn't even noticed in all of the commotion at the ranch that Buster and Junior were missing too.

Now the goat was bleating loudly, going along with the barking of the dog he could still hear farther up. Hopping from his horse, he ran, letting Buster's voice lead him through the darkness.

"Mark!" he called loudly and he could make out

moaning over the sound of the wind and barking—from the bottom of the ravine.

Grabbing the rope from his saddle, he tied it onto a tree and used it to climb down the short distance to the bottom. As he got there, he could make out the form of Buster lying on top of Mark as they lay on the ground.

"Mark, are you all right?" He dropped to the ground beside him and realized the boy was only wearing a sweater. He looked nearly frozen, only the heat of the dog lying near him keeping him warm. Pulling the jacket from his back, he laid it on him.

"Co-co-old. And I think I hurt my leg." Mark's voice was quiet and hard to make out through the chattering of his teeth as he spoke.

"Here, let me help you up. We need to get you back to the house so you can get warmed up. We'll worry about your leg when we get there." He was already putting his arm behind Mark's shoulders to get him sitting up. As they stood, Buster finally moved from his spot. Immediately, Junior came from the edge where he'd walked down to the bottom of the ravine. The animals started to make the climb back to the top, going over the rocks and ground that jutted out.

Knowing he couldn't get up that way, Harris knew he was going to have to use the rope to climb back out like he'd come down.

"I'm going to climb up, then throw this rope

back down. Do you think you can get it tied around your waist so I can pull you up?" Mark was wobbling and Harris hoped he hadn't hit his head in the fall.

"I can try."

Once he got up to the top, he flung the rope back down, yelling for Mark to grab it. He could feel the rope moving as the boy tied it around his waist, then called to say he was ready.

The wind bit through his shirt and the wetness slithered down as the snow melted where it touched the heat from his body. He was going to be soaked through and he still had to get Mark home.

He pulled on the rope, cringing every time he heard the thump as Mark hit the side of the bank. When he finally got him up over the edge, he sat hard on the ground to catch his breath.

"Mark, what were you thinking? Why would you run away like this? Your sister is out of her mind with worry. I thought you'd have more sense than this." The wind blew loudly between them, whipping hard pellets of ice onto their cheeks.

Buster and Junior were on either side of Mark, obviously ready to carry him home themselves if they had to.

"Answer me, Mark. You're a man now, so you need to start acting like one!" His anger bubbled over as he realized how close the boy had come to dying out here. Patience would have been devastated.

"Because I knew you'd be mad. Just like you are." The words acted like water on a flame, quickly extinguishing the anger that had boiled over.

He got up, putting his hand out to pull Mark to his feet. "I'm not mad, Mark, but I was worried. You could have frozen to death out here."

Mark couldn't put weight on his one leg, crying out in pain as he tried. Harris lifted Mark's arm over his shoulder and helped him get to the horse. Hoisting Mark up first, Harris flung his leg up behind him in the saddle and started the horse moving toward home.

They rode back in silence, with Buster and Junior following beside them. The snow and wind never let up, pushing against them and threatening to consume them.

Finally, seeing the glow of a light in the distance, Harris smiled, knowing Patience would have made sure a lantern was lit near the door. Thinking about her there waiting, and likely making herself sick with worry, he hurried toward home.

Watching her run out the door, his heart leaped from his chest. Remembering the tears in her eyes when he'd left, he was glad to be able to give her brother back to her.

He helped Mark dismount, staying back so they could have their reunion.

A strange feeling overcame Harris as he watched her hug her brother to her chest, while she looked up and met his eyes. The tears flowed down her cheeks but the smile she sent him showed how thankful she was.

While he watched, he wished she was hugging him the same way and he suddenly realized making her happy was the one thing he wanted to do more than anything else in the world.

Even risking his own life to go out in a snow-storm to save her fool-headed brother.

CHAPTER 18

"Patience, let go. I can manage by myself. I don't need you in here." Mark was pushing her hands away as she tried to help him get the shirt over his head. Harris had followed them into the house to pull the big tub out they used for bathing and put it in Mark's room.

Patience had boiled water, while Harris ran to the well to get more buckets to fill the tub. She felt bad, Harris was soaked through—having given his warm jacket to Mark. She knew he was likely in need of this warm bath as much as her brother.

"Mark, I know you're older now and don't want your sister here while you undress, but how do you plan on getting in that tub yourself with your leg like that?"

He still wasn't able to put any weight on his leg without pain. Harris said they'd have to head in to

Abilene and see a doctor as soon as the snow lifted.

"I'll wait until Harris is back to help me," he grumbled. She knew he was feeling shame over what he did but she had to make sure he realized the extent of what he'd done wrong.

"Fine, he'll be back from putting the horse away in a moment. Meanwhile, do you want to tell me why you ran away like that?"

She tried to keep the anger and worry from her voice.

He sat slouched with the jacket still wrapped around his shoulders as he shivered on the chair in his room.

Finally, he lifted his eyes and looked at her. "Because I knew I'd be in trouble. I left so he wouldn't send us both away."

Her heart plummeted. "What do you mean? Why would he send us both away?"

He rolled his eyes as though, he was exasperated that she couldn't understand. "Well, letting a camel loose in the middle of Kansas isn't a good thing. I knew he'd be mad. And I also know you two still aren't married for real, so I knew he could send us both away easily. I figured with me gone, he wouldn't want to get rid of you on your own."

She didn't even know what to say.

"Mark, you can't be serious. Harris wouldn't have sent you away over something like that."

"You should listen to your sister. If you'd have just come and told me what had happened, I could have helped you find Annie. Turns out, she wasn't far away anyway and was returned to her pen within minutes of me heading out to look for you."

The two of them had been so caught up in talking to each other, they hadn't even heard Harris come in. He poured another bucket of water into the metal tub. Steam still hung in the air above as it mixed with the already boiled water.

"I wouldn't have sent anyone away. I'd think you'd know me better than that by now."

Mark kept his head hung, obviously afraid to look up at Harris.

"Here, let me help you get in this water before it cools off so I can go get changed out of these wet clothes." Harris's eyes met hers as he motioned for her to leave the room.

She went out to put another pot of water on to boil. Harris would need something warm to drink.

Sitting in the chair beside the fire, she dropped her head into her hands. Mark was so afraid that Harris would treat them just as badly as the Thompsons had done, he'd been willing to leave to protect them from him.

Would he ever get over the mistrust and pain he held in his heart?

All of the worry she'd had while Harris was out searching for Mark made her slump. That, combined with the sorrow she felt over the stolen innocence for herself and her brother, made tears flow down her cheeks. Her shoulders shook as she sobbed while the pain of the past and the relief at Mark being all right overtook her.

She'd held everything in for so long.

Patience heard Harris come into the room and she lifted her eyes to look at him, desperately trying to bring her anguish under control. She didn't want him to see her like this. She vaguely noticed he'd already gone and changed into dry clothes as he reached down and pulled her up, taking her in his arms.

He didn't say a word, just holding her as his hand stroked her hair. Being held in his arms, she realized how much she never wanted to leave his embrace.

For the first time in as long as she could remember, she felt safe.

When she didn't have any tears left to cry, she pulled back and looked up into eyes she almost didn't recognize through the coldness of his gaze.

"What happened to his back?" His voice was choked and anger was just below the surface.

She was confused for a moment, then she realized he must have seen the scars on Mark's back from the many beatings he'd endured over his young lifetime.

"The Thompsons weren't good people, Harris."

She didn't want to tell him everything, not sure how he'd react when he learned of the life they'd lived before.

She kept her eyes turned up, watching as the muscles in his jaw clenched. He was looking past her, wrestling with an anger she could feel shaking his entire body. "Did they whip you too?" This time his voice was low and he kept his eyes looking over her shoulder.

She swallowed, afraid to answer. Shame rippled through her body as she remembered the times the whip had broken through her skin. So many times she wanted to take Mark and leave but she didn't know where to go. The guilt she carried, knowing she was the eldest and should have taken care of them, ate at her soul.

When she didn't reply, he looked down. His arms were still around her, one hand on her back while the other held tightly to her shoulder. He wanted an answer.

Nodding, a low guttural sound come from him that shook his chest held against hers. He pulled her tight again, pressing her head into his shoulder.

They stood in each other's arms, listening to the sound of the wind whipping around the house outside, while the fire crackled beside them. Finally, he released her enough to pull back and look down at her.

Before she knew what was happening, his head

was moving closer and as his lips touched hers, her heart tumbled in her chest. A fire was ignited as she felt the heat of his breath while his hands caressed her back.

The stubble against her skin burned as he pulled her even tighter against him. She brought her hand up to touch his cheek, while her other hand pushed through the back of his hair. He groaned as her hand touched his skin.

He pulled back again and she instantly felt cold where he'd been. Opening her eyes, she watched as his shoulders heaved, his breathing coming in sharp gasps.

He lifted his hand and gently started to caress the skin on her jaw, slowly making soothing circles as he made his way down her neck. His eyes were watching hers, asking her if she wanted him to stop.

Licking her lips, she waited, unsure what to do next. She gasped as he reached behind her and swung her legs off the floor, holding her in his arms.

"No one will ever hurt you again, Patience. That's a promise."

His lips came back down and as he carried her across the room, she was sure her heart would burst with love.

Somehow, she knew he meant every word.

CHAPTER 19

She watched as Dr. Hastings dipped the cloths into the plaster mixture, then wrapped them around Mark's leg. The doctor said his leg had been broken just above the ankle, so he was applying a cast to help it heal. She wasn't sure the doctor was completely sober as he'd stumbled in to the room earlier smelling like he'd come straight from the saloon up the street but he was better than nothing.

They'd come in to Abilene first thing this morning, the snow and wind finally stopping enough for them to bundle up and make the trip to town. There was no doctor in Romance, so since they'd had to come all this way, Harris had gone out to stock up on some supplies while they waited for the cast to set. The doctor said it would be a few hours at least.

Standing to stretch, she decided to step outside for some fresh air. The smell of the medicines and ointments in the doctor's office was starting to make her head spin. Stepping out into the cool air, she pulled her jacket tight around her shoulders. The wind and snow had stopped but there was still a crisp chill in the air.

Leaning against the doorframe, she watched as the people of Abilene carried about with their lives. Wagons and horses made their way through the streets as people skirted past, trying not to get caught under the wheels as they crossed.

"So, Harris has managed to convince you to stay. Thought you'd be long gone by now."

She cringed as she heard Dirk's voice. Turning to look at him, she raised an eyebrow and crossed her arms in front of her. "I would have thought you'd be long gone from here too. Or are you still hanging around waiting for the chance to win the ranch?" She wasn't sure where she'd gotten the nerve to speak to him like that but something about the man had always irked her.

He laughed loudly. "Well, looks like you've got pretty uppity now that you're the lady of the man with the biggest fortune in Kansas." He moved around to stand right in front of her, his arm reaching up to rest beside her on the doorframe.

"You might want to listen up, little lady. You

don't need to think you've got one up on me. Do you truly think Harrison Winchester will be content to stay with you after he's got the deed to that ranch?" He laughed cruelly as he stepped to the side, bringing his hand back down.

"Take a look across the street. Do you see that?" His chin motioned to a couple standing in front of the mercantile. The man had his arms around the woman as she held on to his arms. She knew instantly it was Harris by the jacket he wore but she couldn't see who the lady was.

Her heart fell as the woman finally turned enough for her to see the blonde curls sticking out from beneath her bonnet. Jane was smiling up at Harris as Patience stood, unable to move, watching while Harris held the other woman in his arms.

"I assure you, Jane won't stop until she gets her hands on that fortune. I've known her my whole life. She'd never give me the time of day until I wrote and told her I was inheriting all that money." He stared across at the other couple. "As much as it angers me to see her with Winchester, I thought I should warn you. You're about to become just another one of the many women Harrison Winchester has cast off to the side. In case you hadn't noticed, Jane is just about the most beautiful woman this side of the Pacific Ocean and Harrison has the name, and now the money, that every woman wants."

She stood unable to move, swallowing hard to fight back the tears that were threatening to fall. Last night, she'd given herself to him, believing theirs would be a true marriage made in love.

She knew without a doubt she loved him but from what she was standing here watching, she realized he didn't feel the same way.

"Anything he's done or said to make you believe otherwise, I assure you, sweetheart, it's only been to keep you here for the six months so he can win this fortune."

Her heart was screaming it couldn't be true but her eyes couldn't erase what she'd seen.

"Everything all right here, ma'am?" A man's voice broke through her thoughts. She turned her head to look at him, struggling to focus through the tears. A tall man with a hat stood in front of her and he was glaring at Dirk. He turned back to look at her and smiled. "This man bothering you?"

Dirk laughed again, then pushed himself away from the wall. "Nothing that concerns you."

The other man tilted his head and raised an eyebrow as he pinned Dirk under his gaze. "I'll let the lady here tell me that herself, if you don't mind." He tipped his hat as he looked at her. "My name's Brooks Vaughn. And if this man is troubling you, just say the word."

Dirk took in a sharp breath. "Brooks Vaughn?" His voice sounded strangled and he quickly started to back away. "I was just leaving anyway." He practically turned and ran in the other direction.

She noticed the dimple in the other man's cheek as he smiled down at her, shaking his head. "Sure hope I didn't scare him off."

"Brooks, good to see you. Thanks for helping my wife out. I saw Dirk over here and figured he'd be up to no good." Harris came up behind Brooks to stand beside her.

"Is everything all right?" He directed the question at her.

She put a smile on her face, unwilling to let anyone see how much she was hurting. "Yes, I'm fine. Thank you, Mr. Vaughn, for coming to my rescue." She put her hand out to the other man.

"Well, I might have owed him one." He bowed over and placed a kiss on the back of her hand before he turned his gaze to Harris. "I'd heard you got yourself married too but find it hard to believe someone as pretty as this lady here would ever let herself be tied to the likes of you."

Brooks slapped Harris on the shoulder, then turned. She watched as he walked over to a wagon with two women sitting in it just up the street. She still couldn't let her eyes look at Harris.

"We can stay in town tonight if you'd like. It's going to be dark by the time Mark's cast is ready. I could take you to a restaurant for something to eat and maybe we could have a chance to spend some time alone."

Turning to face him, she finally met his eyes. She wanted to believe everything Dirk had said were lies but her head couldn't think straight.

"No, Harris. I just want to go home."

CHAPTER 20

Harris threw the straw into a pile, taking his frustration out on the fork in his hands. Tucker came over and sniffed at his ankles, then trotted back and started to drink the water he'd poured into the bucket for the animal. As he cleaned the pen, his thoughts went to Patience.

He didn't know what had gotten into her but he had his suspicions that Dirk was behind it. She swore he didn't tell her anything she didn't already know, but the way she said it led him to believe there was more she wasn't saying.

He'd hoped to get rooms in town so he could take her out and have the chance to tell her what he felt. He wasn't good at talking about his feelings and since they always seemed to be interrupted at home, he'd thought a night on their own would be perfect.

He'd stopped at the mercantile and found a ring they had that would be perfect for her. They'd been married hastily when she'd arrived and he hadn't ever planned on making it a permanent arrangement, so had never bought a ring. He was hoping to take the chance to let her know he wanted her to stay and make theirs a true marriage.

And after the other night, he'd believed she would feel the same.

Something had happened in town to change her mind. She'd barely spoken a word on the way home in the darkness, refusing to move closer to him for warmth even though he could feel her shivering. When they'd arrived home, she'd quietly gone to her room, closing the door behind her.

All she would say to him is that she needed time to think.

He'd spent the night racking his mind to figure out what he'd done wrong.

Stepping outside, he breathed in the cool air. The snow had all melted from the storm the other night but the air still held some crispness. The sun was bright, so he shielded his eyes as he turned to head to the next pen.

Henry had already been around to introduce him to his daughter and her husband who'd shown up yesterday from Idaho. He knew Henry didn't get to see them often and was glad to see the older man so happy. At the moment, they were going around the ranch, seeing the new animals they'd acquired since the couple had visited last.

When he'd met Henry's daughter Anne, he thought he noticed something vaguely familiar about her but he knew it wasn't likely he'd have ever met her. Hearing the sound of hooves pounding up the long lane leading to the ranch, he walked toward the house to see who it was coming to visit this early in the day.

Lewis? What was he doing here? "You're an awful long way from Abilene. And I know you aren't here just to visit because you were missing me. I just saw you yesterday in town."

His friend hopped down from his horse, striding toward him with a grim look on his face. "No, it's not a social visit, Harris. I don't think we have much time, so I'd like to talk to you and Patience together."

Harris's heart filled with dread. He hadn't seen Lewis like this before. "Well, she's not really talking to me at the moment but I'm sure she'd be willing to listen to you." He started to walk to the house but he caught the raised eyebrow in his direction.

"So, she's come to her senses then and realized she could do a lot better then you?"

He kept walking, shaking his head at how quick Lewis could go from deadly serious to teasing him mercilessly about his apparent lack of worth to offer Patience.

As he opened the door, his eyes fell on Patience standing by the stove. She was stirring something she'd set on the fire and the house was filled with the smells of the lunch she was making for the men in the bunkhouse.

He'd felt a strange sense of pride at how well she'd settled in, being able to feed the men much better than they'd ever eaten. They all were smitten with her, sure she'd hung the moon in the sky. She treated them all kindly and always made sure they were well fed.

The smile she always wore had won over the hearts of even the most grizzled ranch hands.

But when she looked at him now, the smile was gone. He wanted to run over and grab her in his arms, demanding she tell him what was wrong. He wanted to fix it. Making it worse, her face light up with a smile as Lewis come in behind him.

Apparently, it was just him she wasn't willing to smile at.

"Lewis, what are you doing here? I have some water boiling, so sit down and let me get you a warm drink." Harris noticed she didn't even acknowledge him.

"I'm afraid I'm not coming with the best news." He looked at Harris and that feeling of dread overtook him again.

"I had a visit early this morning from a couple named Andrea and Daniel Thompson."

Harris whipped his head toward the sound of china shattering, then ran to where Patience stood next to the table, her hands frozen in front of her where she'd held the cup. When he got to her, he put his hands on her shoulders, feeling her tremble. Her eyes were wide, seeming too large for her face, as she finally looked at him.

"They can't hurt you, Patience. I promised and I meant it." He put his arms around her shoulders, leading her to sit down in her chair. He crouched down in front of her, taking her hands in his.

"I'm not letting them anywhere near you."

Harris looked up at Lewis who'd walked over beside them. "What did they say?"

"They stormed into my office, saying they knew Patience and Mark had got off the train here. They never told me how they found them but they were demanding to know where they are now. And telling me I had to arrest Patience."

"Arrest her for what?" Harris leaped to his feet, fury consuming him.

Lewis looked at Patience who was sitting looking at her folded hands in her lap. "For stealing money from them."

Her voice was quiet and he almost thought he didn't hear her right. By now, the noise had brought

Mark hobbling from his bedroom. Harris met the boy's gaze above her bowed head.

"Patience, you used that money to bring me with you. I won't let you take the blame for that." He stood up as straight as his cast leg would allow him while he tried to hold the wall for balance. "Mr. Kinkaid, if you are going to arrest anyone, arrest me. It was me who took the money."

"Mark, don't!" Patience stood and ran to her brother. "I took that money and I'd do it again in a heartbeat to get you away from there."

Harris stomped over to them. "Why didn't you just use the money I'd sent you? I sent you plenty of money you could have used for another ticket."

She turned and lifted her chin as she met his eyes. "Because it wasn't my money and I didn't want to start our marriage by me taking advantage of your kindness or your trust in sending me the money for a ticket. I figured after everything we'd done for the Thompsons, they owed us the money."

"I'm not arresting anyone," Lewis interrupted. "But I wanted to give you the heads up. I saw them talking to Dirk after I kicked them out of my office, so I have no doubt they'll be headed this way soon."

"Stay here." Harris cursed as he turned from Patience and made his way to the door. "And, Lewis, you stay with her until I get back. Make sure they stay put. I'm getting Henry and the other men."

"Harris, what are you doing?" He could hear the strain of fear in her voice.

"I'm going to make sure the Thompsons know they aren't welcome anywhere near my wife ever again."

CHAPTER 21

She moved to the stove in a daze. What was going to happen to her and Mark now? The fact remained that she had stolen the money from the Thompsons and she knew they weren't the type of people to just let that go. She'd seen what they did to people who tried to cheat them out of what they were owed.

Even though she'd known at the time what she was doing was wrong, the happiness she'd seen on Mark's face these past few weeks made it worth it. She'd always known deep down it would likely catch up to her and they would find her but she hadn't let herself think about it too much.

Now they were here and she knew they'd try to make Lewis arrest her.

She crouched down and started to pick up the pieces of china she'd broken. "Just let me get this cleaned up, Lewis, and I'll make you a cup of coffee."

"That's all right, Patience, I don't need anything." She stood up and carried the pieces of china to the ash can.

He was leaning against the wall by the door watching her. "You know Harris isn't going to let them do anything to you or Mark. You do realize that, don't you?"

She looked at him as he stood with arms crossed, guarding the door. She wondered if he was keeping anyone from getting in or actually making sure she didn't try to get out.

Looking out the window, the sun shone against the blue of the sky. Some of the animals moved about in their pens and she smiled as Tucker played with a leaf in his enclosure. He was obviously feeling much better.

"I don't know what to think or believe anymore, Lewis. I may be his wife in name but I'm not sure he will care too much one way or another what happens with the Thompsons."

The sound of a quiet laugh met her ears, so she turned to look at Lewis.

He was shaking his head at her. "Patience, can't you see what's right in front of your eyes? How could you think he won't care?"

The vision of Jane in his arms tore through her memory.

Lewis walked over to her. "I've known Harris a long time, almost my whole life. And I've never seen him like he is with you. You've done something to him that no other woman has ever been able to do."

She wrinkled her eyebrows together. "I find it very difficult to believe I could have that much of an effect on any man. As much as I'd like to believe we have a future together, I know there are other women out there who can offer him more than I can."

"Patience, I've always thought you were the smartest woman I knew but sometimes you can be so foolish. Even I can see that Harris is in love with you."

This time it was her brother's voice that she heard as he hobbled closer and sat down at the table.

"And the only reason I'm not worried right now is because even I know Harris isn't going to let anything happen to either of us. I don't know why you can't see that too."

She wanted to but how could she tell them what she'd seen yesterday?

"Yesterday, while Mark was getting his leg set, Harris came to my office. He told me to find the Thompsons. He wanted to make them pay for what he said they'd done to you and Mark. He never told me what happened but he said he'd spend his entire inheritance from Elijah if he had to, to make sure they paid somehow." Lewis looked out the window. "Guess they saved me the effort of finding them."

She hadn't realized he'd gone to see Lewis. Everything was so jumbled in her mind, nothing made sense.

She'd believed Harris had feelings for her and as she remembered the other night and the love they'd shared, her heart skipped a beat. She would never have given herself to a man if she didn't believe he cared for her.

Maybe what she saw with Jane wasn't what she imagined. Her stomach rolled as she realized she hadn't been fair to Harris. She'd never given him the chance to explain, letting the thoughts in her head think only the worst. He'd never given her any reason to believe otherwise but she'd let her imagination get carried away.

All because she didn't believe she was worthy of a man like Harris.

Looking back out the window, Harris was striding back toward the house, with all of the ranch hands behind him. Henry was walking beside him with another couple she didn't recognize.

Her whole body warmed as she realized all of these people were coming here to fight for her. They weren't going to let anything happen to her or Mark. And Harris was leading them, determined to keep her safe.

She wondered if this was what it felt like to have family who cared about you?

Patience saw a flicker from the corner of her eye and the people walking toward the house all turned in that direction. Moving her head closer to the glass to see what had gotten their attention, she saw a wagon make its way up the road, being led by Dirk on horseback.

Her stomach churned when she recognized Daniel Thompson sitting in the seat.

She turned and walked to the door as Mark tried to stand. Lewis went over and helped him, putting his arm around his back so he could walk.

"I'm not letting him face them without me. I'm the one who stole the money and I'm the one they want to see. But this time, I'm not afraid of them." Lewis nodded and opened the door. The three of them walked to the crowd of people standing waiting for the wagon to come up the lane.

She walked over and smiled at Harris as she took his hand. He looked down at her with confusion, then returned the smile and squeezed her hand.

"Don't worry. They won't hurt you."

She nodded. "I know."

As the wagon pulled up, Daniel spotted her and started shouting, "You little floozy, you think you can steal my money and get away with it? Running off without so much as a thank you for all of the years we cared for you!"

His voice brought shivers to her spine as all the memories of past fears and hurts returned. Her brother limped up beside her and took her other hand. Lewis stood on the other side of him, presenting a united force.

As they waited for the wagon to come to a complete stop, Dirk's smug face glared at Harris. "Looks like you're about to lose your ranch, Harris. Can't stay married to a fugitive. She'll be locked up before the sun goes down."

Henry stepped forward. "I told you, Dirk, you aren't welcome on this land."

Dirk just laughed. "Doesn't matter what you think, old man. The will states that she has to stay on this ranch and if she doesn't, anyone else can get married and step in."

One of the other ranch hands stepped forward. "Dirk, if I were you, I'd turn and leave now. I found some interesting items you left behind in your rush to leave." The man turned to Henry. "You might want to check in his tack box. You might just find some more traps that were ready to be put out on the ranch."

Everyone had been watching Dirk closely, so no one had noticed the Thompson's wagon come to a stop or the couple step down until a woman's voice spoke up.

"Andrea Thompson?" The woman who'd been

with Henry stepped forward. Patience hadn't met her yet but she knew it must be his daughter.

Patience watched as the Thompsons turned to see who had called her name, probably unsure how anyone would recognize them all the way out here. Something flickered in Andrea's face the moment she saw the other woman. Her face went whiter than the snow that had fallen only days ago.

Patience couldn't understand what was happening. Henry's daughter turned and looked at her with tears in her eyes as she met her stare.

"Patience?" The voice sounded familiar as she spoke her name. How did she know who she was? Henry must have told her about her. "I knew the name wasn't common but I thought it must have just been a coincidence. Is it really you?"

The woman was walking toward her and the Thompsons were struggling to get back into the wagon.

What was going on? Why would they be trying to flee?

"Matthew?" The woman was now looking at Mark.

"No ma'am, sorry. My name's Mark."

Something tugged at her memory. This woman looked familiar. *What was it?*

Suddenly, the dreams she'd had at night burst into her thoughts. The woman's face—it was the woman singing to her in her dreams. She remembered laughing with this woman and having her brush her hair. She even remembered being given a little dog when she was a little girl. His name had been Tucker.

Everything started to spin.

"Ma?" Her voice could barely come out above a whisper as a sob caught in her throat.

CHAPTER 22

Harris was on the wagon before it could move. The Thompsons had clearly tried to get away, hoping the confusion of everything would distract everyone. He grabbed Daniel by the collar and dragged him from the seat. Landing on the ground with a loud thud, Patience cried out as she watched Daniel swing at Harris.

He was no match for the younger man, though, and, within seconds, Harris was on top of him, with his hands tight around the other man's throat.

"You don't deserve to live for what you did to Patience and Mark. And by the sounds of it, you did even more than you've ever had to pay for," he hissed the words loud enough for everyone to hear.

Patience ran over. "Harris, let him go. You don't need to do this. I don't want you to end up in jail for killing him. He's not worth it." She tried to pull his arm to make him let go of Daniel Thompson's face which was turning purple as he struggled to breathe.

But Harris couldn't hear her. His rage had stopped all of his other senses. Andrea was screaming as Lewis grabbed her and dragged her over beside them.

"Harris! Let go. I'll take care of him." Lewis shoved Andrea toward Henry who held her while he physically fought to restrain Harris from going any further.

"Please, Harris, I need you here. Please, just let him go." Patience pleaded, kneeling beside him.

Finally, he looked at her and let his grip go on the man's throat. "He doesn't deserve to live, Patience, for what he's done."

Daniel lay sputtering on the ground as Lewis finally wrestled him upright.

Then he yanked Thompson up and made him face the crowd of people.

Henry's daughter was lying on the ground with her husband kneeling beside her. She had promptly passed out when Patience called her ma. Patience ran over, crouching on the ground by her. The man beside her had tears in his eyes as he looked at Patience.

"Is it really you, Patience? We never thought we'd ever find you," his voice shook with emotion.

Her mother was coming to and, as she opened her eyes, the tears started to fall as she took in

Patience's face leaning over her. She reached her hand up and touched her cheek and Patience knew without a doubt this was the woman from her dreams.

"Ma, I thought you'd died. They told me you both died on the way to Oregon. I couldn't remember much but I had dreams sometimes and I could see your face as you were singing me to sleep at night."

Her ma sat up, pulling her into her arms. "No, you and Matthew were taken from us. We'd stopped at a fort near Idaho one night and the Thompsons, who'd been on the wagon train with us, offered to look after you children while we ran in to pick up more supplies."

She pulled back and looked into Patience's eyes. "When we got back, you were gone."

This time, the man, her pa, spoke, "We stayed in Idaho, determined to find you both, never stopping our search."

"What's going on, Patience?" Mark had hobbled over and his voice shook with confusion and fear.

She stood up, taking her mother's hand to help her to her feet. "Mark, these are our parents. They didn't die on the way to Oregon like the Thompsons told us."

Mark looked back and forth between them all until tears streamed down his cheeks. As their mother threw herself into his arms, Harris had to grab Mark so he didn't fall.

The sound of Andrea Thompson's voice wailing reached her ears. "We couldn't have children of our own. They abandoned them. We just took care of them like any good person would. We couldn't leave them there."

The woman was hysterical, realizing the horrific crime they'd committed had just been uncovered. Patience almost smiled as she watched Buster and Junior walk over to get in on the action. Buster was growling low in his throat, warning the woman she was about to pay if she didn't stop yelling.

Dirk had turned and rode as fast out of the yard as his horse would take him. One of the men ran to grab a horse to follow him but Henry just shook his head. "Let him go. He won't come back around here. He knows if he does he'll have to answer for what he's done." Henry's eyes turned to her. "Besides, he knows he's lost now."

Henry slowly walked toward her. He reached out and took her hands in his. "I'd always known I felt something familiar about you. I couldn't make it out. Now I know, you were my own precious little girl who used to sit on your grandpa's knee. Your grandma loved you dearly and would be beside herself with happiness to know you were back."

Patience swallowed the sob as she watched the

tears flow from his eyes. He hugged her to him and she was sure he'd never let go.

Hearing a ruckus, she pulled back to see what was happening. The men were helping Lewis get the Thompsons' hands tied behind their backs and Patience walked over.

Immediately, Harris was by her side.

Knowing she had the backing of everyone, Patience felt the need to confront them. "You took everything from us. You took two innocent children and ripped them from a loving family to spend their years working as your servants for nothing. We didn't think we had anyone else."

"You ungrateful wench. We gave you a roof over your heads and food in your bellies. Without us, you'd have died." Daniel was pulling against the man holding him.

Harris grabbed him by the scruff of his shirt again, lifting his feet from the ground. "You're just lucky there are witnesses around here because what I would rather do to you right now would send me straight to hell with you. Now get out of my sight and you better spend your remaining days thinking long and hard about what you've done. If I ever see you again, I don't care if there are any witnesses, you'll pay for the wrongs you've done."

He pushed Daniel hard, making the man sprawl awkwardly on the ground as he spun and took Patience's hand to lead her away. Immediately,

Buster went over and bared his teeth, forcing the man to stay put.

She left her past lying on the ground with Daniel and let Harris lead her away. This man was giving her the future.

CHAPTER 23

The crackling of the fire broke the silence between them as they sat in the chairs beside the fireplace. Everything that had happened today seemed so unreal. Any doubts she had about Harris not caring about her had quickly been erased.

Whatever happened between him and Jane wasn't important anymore.

She'd spent the day getting to know her parents again and finding out that Mark's real name was Matt. Apparently, the Thompsons had known she was old enough to know her name already but since Mark had been just a baby, they'd changed his.

Lewis had taken a couple of the men from the ranch and escorted the Thompsons back to Abilene. He said he'd personally make sure they were locked up and paid for everything they'd done.

All those years apart, taken from them.

Knowing the grief her parents had felt while spending their days trying to find them again, and never giving up hope, broke her heart.

All day, while her family worked through the questions and spent time catching up, Harris had stayed back, letting her have this time with them. She felt terrible knowing how awful she'd been to him yesterday and this morning. She was desperate to get him alone and tell Harris how she felt about him.

It was time to let go of her insecurity. She'd just found out how fast everything could be taken from you and she couldn't ever live with herself if that happened.

Before she could find the words, Harris was standing and coming toward her. He put his hand out and helped her to stand in front of him. He held her arms, finally lifting one hand to brush the hair back from her cheek.

"Patience, I'm sorry for what you had to live through. But if I'm being completely honest, I'm not sorry that because of it, you felt the need to get away by answering an advertisement from a man needing a wife. A complete stranger who could have been just as horrible to you as what you were running from."

"Harris, I knew nothing could be that bad."

He brought his finger up to her lips and shook his head.

"Just let me talk. I'm not good at this kind of thing because, the truth is, I've never felt like this about anyone before in my life. And I don't even understand what's happened to me. One minute, all I cared about was getting my fortune and I didn't care what I had to do to get it. I planned on getting the wife to fulfill that part of the terms, then send her on her way." He swallowed hard and she was finding it hard to breathe at the intensity of his gaze as he kept his eyes on hers.

"I never meant to fall in love."

Her heart almost beat right out of her chest. She was sure her whole body was about to burst with the happiness she was feeling.

Patience felt a tear escape and she hurried to wipe it away. The emotions of the day were catching up to her.

He leaned in and kissed it away before she could.

"I don't know what you've done to me, Patience, but I want you to stay with me and I want us to have a future together."

His fingers were caressing her arm and the other hand was slowly rubbing her cheek.

"Harris, I know you could have any other woman you wanted but I'm so glad you've chosen me. I promise I will do everything I can to make sure you don't regret asking me to come and marry you. I may not be as pretty as Jane but I'll do everything I can to make you happy."

His fingers stopped moving, and he furrowed his eyebrows together as he looked at her. "Jane? Why would you bring her up?"

She felt her cheeks burn. "I'm sorry. It's just that, the other day in town, I saw you holding her across the street and I knew maybe..." How could she finish what she was trying to say when she didn't even know anymore what that was?

His eyes widened and a smile started to creep across his face. "Is that why you were so mad at me? I couldn't figure out what I'd done."

"It doesn't matter, Harris. It's none of my business..." He reached out and took hold of her chin, lifting her eyes to stay on his.

"Patience, Jane has nothing compared to you. All you saw that day was her doing a pathetic attempt at pretending to slip on the walkway, forcing me to have to catch her. I'm sure she knew the exact moment you'd be watching." He shook his head.

"There is no other woman I'd want to hold in my arms, than the one I'm holding right now." His voice had grown husky as he brought his thumb up to gently stroke her lips.

She was sure her heart was going to stop beating as he brought his head down, taking her lips with his. He pulled her in closer, moving his lips in time with every beat of her heart.

When he finally pulled back, she felt like her legs would give out beneath her as she looked up into the face staring back at her.

"I love you, Harris. I'm sure I've loved you since I stepped off the train and saw the kindness in your eyes. I somehow knew you were the one person who could give me a future."

Harris stepped back and reached down into his pocket. When he brought his hand out, he held the most beautiful ring she'd ever seen. He took her hand and lifted it, placing the ring on her finger.

"I never gave you the proper wedding but I promise, I will give you all the love in my heart every day for the rest of our lives."

He lifted her in his arms and smiled down at her. She wrapped her arms around his neck and let her head lean into his chest as he carried her to his room. She felt it rumble as he spoke.

"I never could have imagined just how much I had at stake when I gambled on winning this ranch. But I would trade it all if it meant I'd have to give you up. In my heart, I know now, you're the fortune I've been searching for my whole life."

SPECIAL SNEAK PEEK AT BOOK THREE: A LAWMAN'S REWARD

Available Now for Pre-order!

CHAPTER 1

"Well, you're in luck. My dear husband and I run the Merchants Hotel right on the main street in Abilene. We have a room just for young teachers who are brave enough to try their hand at civilizing the children of this town. Your room is paid for by the parents who pay your wages. It's not much, but you have a roof over your head, a warm bed to sleep in, and meals prepared for you in the small restaurant downstairs."

Lydia couldn't believe her luck at riding the stagecoach with the proprietor of the hotel she'd be staying in. She hadn't sent word ahead to say she'd be coming back to Abilene yet, so her brother wouldn't know to meet her.

She smiled as she looked out the window and started to see some of the familiar sights of the small town that had grown up around her since she was a little girl. Abilene hadn't been much when they were kids and, in fact, had only started out as a stagecoach stop named Mud Creek when was about six. Over the years, the name had been changed to Abilene, and Kansas had since become a state.

At the time, she didn't really pay much attention to everything that was happening, other than she knew more people were moving to the area and the town was getting bigger. After spending the past few months at the Kansas Normal School getting her teacher's training, she'd learned more about the history of her area.

Abilene was now a bustling cow town and had become a bit rough around the edges with people passing through and causing trouble. The last teacher in town had run off within only a few weeks of taking the job. It wasn't a town that many women wanted to live in on their own.

But Lydia had grown up around here and everyone knew her brother, Brooks. At one time, he'd been a well-known gambler who'd had his own share of trouble until he'd found a woman to marry and settle down with. People still knew of his name around here and she knew people wouldn't want to mess with him, so she figured she'd be safer than most women might be.

Not to mention the fact that her brother's best friend was Lewis Kinkaid, one of the top lawmen of the town. She knew that since the town had become more wild with the drifters and cowboys passing through, there'd been many other lawmen who'd come and gone, working alongside Lewis. But he'd stayed, determined he wouldn't let the ruffians drive him away.

Her heart did a little flutter as her thoughts drifted to him. For as long as she'd known Lewis, she'd been attracted to him. His dark blond hair and the touch of stubble that always covered his strong jaw drew her eyes but truthfully, it was his kind and caring personality that had always appealed to her the most.

He was the kind of man you knew you could depend on.

But she wasn't foolish enough to believe a man like him would ever be interested in her, so she'd never let anyone know of her feelings.

She'd been living on the farm with her brother ever since their parents died many years ago and he'd looked after her. But once Brooks had fallen in love and married, she'd known she couldn't stay with the newlywed couple as they started their new life together. So she'd packed her bags to go to teacher's college, never believing she'd be coming back here to teach.

The creaking of the springs in the bouncy stage-coach filled the air as the dust settled around the people inside. It was late in the year but there was still some warmth in the sun as it peeked in through the windows. She could see the outline of the town in the distance and her whole body felt warm knowing she was back home. Soon, she'd see her brother and his wife Fiona who'd become one of her best friends.

Her heart was beating double time, though, because she also knew she'd soon be seeing the man she'd thought about every day since she'd left.

She jumped as the sound of the bugle alerted the station they were arriving. She gave a nervous laugh as she brought her hand up to her chest, smiling across at Mrs. Malloy. "Goodness, that startled me. I was deep in thought, I guess."

Mrs. Malloy patted her knee. "My Harold will be waiting and he can help you get your belongings moved over to the hotel. Oh, I can't tell you how happy I am, knowing you'll be staying with us. I will enjoy the company, that's for sure."

The stagecoach bounced into town and Lydia immediately saw the familiar sights of people milling everywhere she looked, horses riding down the street, dodging wagons that bumped through the ruts. She smiled to herself as she went past the sheriff's office and her breath caught in her throat when the man himself came out the front door, watching as the stagecoach made its way into town.

He was looking right at her, so she waved through the open window, wondering if he'd even see her. A smile lit up his face and as the stage moved past to head around the corner, he jumped down from the stairs, onto the street to follow them.

She tried to ignore the clenching of her stomach as her nerves caused everything, even her skin, to tingle. But he seemed happy to see her.

As the coach stopped with one last bounce forward, she patted at her skirts, trying to get some of the dust and wrinkles out from the trip here from the school in Emporia. The seats lurched forward, indicating the driver had stepped down and, within seconds, the door was being opened.

"Lydia Vaughn. I thought that was you but Brooks hadn't mentioned you'd be back in town yet. I thought for sure you'd taken off for greener and much more civilized pastures."

Lewis's smooth voice reached her ears and she smiled out as he reached in to take her hand and help her step outside.

"That's because I haven't told him. I thought I'd surprise him."

He still held her hand as he helped her step away from the stagecoach and up onto the wooden sidewalk. She was wearing gloves but she could feel the skin beneath the fabric warming from his touch.

"Let me get your bags and I'll take you out to the farm so you can surprise him."

"No, that's fine, Lewis. Thank you. I'm actually staying here in town at the Merchants Hotel. I'm the new teacher." She grinned at the shocked look on his face.

"Why would you come back to this rough and tumble town to teach when you could have gone anywhere else in the country?"

She gave a small laugh as she looked around, avoiding his gaze. If he saw the truth in her eyes, she'd be mortified.

"I figured this town needed someone used to the less civilized residents and happenings, so when I was told there was an opening here, I decided there's no better place than home."

She brought her eyes back up to his and smiled. "Besides, now that Brooks is married, I might just have some little ones to bounce on my knee soon. I wouldn't want to miss out on that. He's the only family I have left."

Lewis gave a loud laugh. "I feel for poor Fiona when that happens. She'll have two children to look after."

Lydia chuckled and gave him a gentle tap on the arm. "Lewis, you know Brooks doesn't act like a child...all the time." They both laughed at the familiar, inside joke.

"Well, I'll help you get your bags to the hotel then." He walked over to the driver and helped the man take the bags down. Lydia smiled as she watched him working.

"My, I've never known Mr. Kinkaid to be so

attentive to anyone. He's always been very kind, and I know he's well liked around here, but he sure seems happy to see you, my dear."

Mrs. Malloy gave her a wink, then turned to give the older man a hug who'd come up behind them. "Oh, Harold, I missed you terribly." She watched the couple embrace and felt a sadness as she wondered if she'd ever have that kind of love for herself.

When they were done, she pulled the man over to meet Lydia. "Harold, this young lady is Lydia Vaughn. She's been at teaching school in Emporia for the past few months but she's from right here in Abilene. She'd already left for school when we arrived to take over the hotel."

The man took Lydia's hand and smiled at her as he shook it.

"She's agreed to come back here and be the schoolteacher for our town, so she'll be staying with us."

"It's nice to meet you, ma'am. I look forward to having you stay with us." His eyes were kind and they held a twinkle that reminded Lydia of her father before her accident.

Shaking her head at the memory, she turned as Lewis came up with her bags. "I'll get Lydia's things over to the hotel, Harold. You look like you'll have your hands full with Edna's." Lewis nodded his head toward the pile of bags at Harold's feet, laughing as he led Lydia down the street toward the hotel.

"So, did you have fun staying in Emporia? I figured some young man would come along and sweep you off your feet and I'd be hearing you'd run off to get married."

She rolled her eyes in his direction. "It was fun and I did meet a lot of new people while I was there. But as for getting swept off my feet, I don't expect that to be happening any time soon." She looked down at the ground, hoping her limp wasn't too noticeable today. Riding in the stagecoach had aggravated it and she was feeling the stiffness.

Not wanting him to start feeling the pity she knew people felt when they noticed she had difficulty walking, she smiled up at him as he walked beside her. "How about you? Any ladies finally catch your eye?"

He huffed loudly and this time it was him rolling his eyes toward her. "You know I'm not really the settling down type."

Yes, she did know that. He'd made it clear for a long time he wasn't interested in chasing after any woman, even if she'd ever had the courage to let him know she was interested.

She was his friend's sister and not the type of woman to catch a man's eye. Especially not one like Lewis who'd already decided he'd never be tied to a woman.

"I don't like it. It isn't safe in town but she won't listen to reason." Brooks banged his hand onto the desk, making Lewis look up at him with one eyebrow raised.

"Why don't you tell me how you're really feeling?"

"Well this town isn't safe for a woman alone. Trust me, I know." Lewis gave a little laugh to himself as Brooks continued, "I'm expecting you to keep an eye on her, you know."

Lewis leaned back in his chair, looping his fingers behind his head. "What if she doesn't want me keeping an eye on her? She's a big girl, Brooks. She can look after herself."

Of course, he wouldn't ever admit to his friend that he'd already been having the same worries about Lydia and had already planned to keep a close eye on her. He'd worked this town long enough to know how unruly and dangerous it was.

Lydia was an easy target for anyone wanting to take advantage of her too. Her kindness would be seen as weakness, so he was going to have to be extra diligent in keeping her safe. She'd been so excited yesterday when he'd walked her to her new hotel room, talking about how she was ready to teach the children in town and build a life of her own.

He'd offered to ride out to let Brooks and Fiona know she was home but she'd asked him to wait until morning. She said she knew Brooks was going to argue with her about her decision and she was tired after being stuck in the stagecoach all day.

They'd eaten their dinner together in the restaurant below the hotel while she shared stories from her time in Emporia. And he regaled her with tales from what had been going on around here.

As soon as he'd ridden out to tell her brother she was home this morning, Brooks had raced back to town behind him, determined to talk some sense into his sister. Lydia and Fiona had now just walked down to the mercantile, leaving Lewis to try calming Brooks down.

"Hopefully, after a few days of actually being right in the middle of town and seeing what all goes on around here, she'll come to her senses and come back to the farm. There's no reason I can't simply bring her in each day to the school if she's still determined to teach here."

"Brooks, you know as well as I do how much of a hassle that would be, especially during the months you need to be working the fields. It's coming up to winter here, so the men drifting through from the cattle drives will be slowing down. It'll mostly be locals and men passing through to work the stock-yards and rails. Hopefully, she'll be all settled in by the time spring comes around and things start to pick up around here again."

The Deputy US Marshal, Tom Smith walked in and went over to sit behind his desk. Since he'd arrived in town at the end of last year, he'd insisted he could run this town with no guns, relying only on his own hands and wit to look after the citizens. He believed Abilene had become too dangerous, so had banned guns within town limits.

He wasn't a popular man with the cowboys and drifters who passed through but he was tough and had proven he could look after the place. He'd had a couple of assassination attempts but survived, so Lewis admired how well he could handle himself.

"Tom, will you tell Brooks his sister, Lydia, will be safe staying in Abilene to teach at the school? "Lewis grinned at Brooks, knowing he'd never argue with a man like Tom "Bear River" Smith.

"I'll make sure Lewis keeps his eye on your sister and if he can't handle the duty, I'll find someone who can." This time it was Tom who grinned at Lewis, knowing how much he didn't like anyone implying he wasn't capable of doing a job he was assigned to.

A flash of skirts caught his eye out the window. He realized the women had come out of the mercantile, their arms piled high with fabrics and other items Lydia planned to use to clean up the school room.

He stood up quickly, grabbing his hat off the hook by his desk and moved outside. Before they could even get across the street to the mercantile, Lewis's stomach tightened as three men approached the women. Lydia and Fiona were laughing and talking to each other, not paying attention to their surroundings as they balanced the items in their arms.

Lydia ran into one of the men who took the opportunity to grab onto her arm, pretending to help her from falling. "A pretty girl like you should really be watching where she's going. There's all kinds of dangerous men around these parts ready to take advantage of a pretty lady."

"Lucky for her, she's got a couple of men who are keeping a close eye on her and won't be letting that happen. But thank you for your concern." Lewis walked right up and made sure the man saw his badge on the front of his vest.

He was almost sure he could hear Brooks

growling behind him and didn't need to be breaking up any fights if he could help it. Reaching out, he took the things out of Lydia's arms, while Brooks reached for his wife's.

"Well, we were just making sure the ladies were safe. Wouldn't have wanted them stepping off the edge of the sidewalk onto the street where they could be trampled by a passing wagon. Or have them run into any of the unsavory people wandering around the town."

Lewis just kept his eyes on the men, nodding to let them know their help was no longer needed.

As they walked past, Brooks turned on Lydia. "This is exactly why you're not staying in town on your own. I won't allow it. I'm still considered your guardian and I say you're coming home with me."

"Brooks, let's walk up to the schoolhouse so we can talk about this without everyone staring at us." People were starting to stop and watch, wondering what the argument on the street was about. Fiona took her husband's arm, smiling up at him and leading him down the street.

The schoolhouse sat on the edge of the town, away from the saloons and other immoral establishments the parents hoped to keep the children away from.

Lewis offered Lydia a smile as they fell in behind Brooks and Fiona. He could see the worry in her eyes about the possibility of Brooks forcing her to live out on the farm with him. Last night, as they'd eaten together, she'd talked about not wanting to be a burden on her brother. She felt so much guilt for everything that had happened over the years and she didn't want him to be responsible for caring for her anymore.

She wanted Brooks to have this time with his new wife and she didn't want to intrude. It was important for her to start making her own life, and that meant living on her own and following the profession she'd been trained for.

Suddenly, he had an idea. "Brooks, I have a suggestion that might just ease your mind a bit."

They'd reached the stairs to the schoolhouse and stopped walking. Brooks turned back to face them, his expression still showing determination. He wasn't backing down on this argument.

"The boardinghouse where I've been living has changed owners and the monthly cost has gone up. I was thinking of looking for a house somewhere in town since I figured I'll likely be staying for a while. How about I get a room in the Merchants Hotel too, so I can be nearby if she needs me? At least until you feel she's safe."

AVAILABLE FEBRUARY 2022

ABOUT THE AUTHOR

USA Today Bestselling Author, Kay P. Dawson writes sweet western romance – the kind that leaves out all of the juicy details and immerses you in a true, heartfelt love story. Growing up pretending she was Laura Ingalls, she's always had a love for the old west and pioneer times. She believes in true love, and finding your happy ever after.

Happily married mom of two girls, Kay has always taught her children to follow their dreams. And, after a breast cancer diagnosis at the age of 39, she realized it was time to take her own advice. She had always wanted to write a book, and she decided that the someday she was waiting for was now.

She writes western historical, contemporary and time travel romance that all transport the reader to a time or place where true love always finds a way.